A Beautiful Place to Die

"We picked up Philip R. Craig's novel along with a stack of others... The next thing we knew, we had finished the book and the others were forgotten. It's that kind of story, effortless to read—thanks to the author's clean, fresh prose—yet memorable for its strong and appealing characters and attractive setting... Ex-cop Jeff Jackson is the kind of guy you'd like to join in a cold Samuel Adams on his comfortable porch. We hope he'll figure into more books from this talented author." *Denver Post*

"Craig does a nice job... He knows the chamber-of-commerce view of the island, and also the dark underside." *Providence Sunday Journal*

"Lets the reader become an islander for a while, discovering that beautiful though it is, the Vineyard has its own problems with drugs and crime... An exciting adventure story." *Houston Post*

"The setting works effectively, with crusty, fish-loving locals providing ambience aplenty... A fine debut for a promising mystery series." *Booklist*

A Beautiful Place to Die

A Martha's Vineyard Mystery

PHILIP R. CRAIG

AVON BOOKS ◆ NEW YORK

AVON BOOKS
A division of
The Hearst Corporation
1350 Avenue of the Americas
New York, New York 10019

Copyright © 1989 by Philip R. Craig
Published by arrangement with Charles Scribner's Sons, Macmillan Publishing Company
Library of Congress Catalog Card Number: 89-10126
ISBN: 0-380-71155-9

First Avon Books Printing: August 1991

AVON TRADEMARK REG. U.S. PAT. OFF. AND IN OTHER COUNTRIES, MARCA REGISTRADA, HECHO EN CANADA

Printed in Canada.

UNV 10   9   8   7   6   5   4   3   2

To my wife,
Shirley Prada Craig,
a Vineyard woman, a daughter of the sea

Special thanks to Toni Chute, giver of wise advice, and Ken Layman, who thought of the ring.

A Beautiful Place to Die

* 1 *

The alarm went off at three-thirty. Outside it was as black as a tax collector's heart. Smart me had stopped at the market the night before for doughnuts, so I was on the road as soon as I filled my thermos with coffee. I rattled through Edgartown without seeing another soul and went on south toward Katama. The air was sharp and dry, and the wind was light from the southwest. Maybe it would blow the bluefish in at last. They were two weeks late, or at least two weeks later than the year before. The heater in the Landcruiser didn't work too well, so I was a bit chilly for the first few miles.

Near the end of the pavement, I passed the condos and the new houses on the right (six big figures last year, six bigger figures this year). Who would want one? Lots of people, of course. This was Martha's Vineyard, after all, that green gem of an island circled by gold, set in a sapphire sea. Some enterprising entrepreneurs in the drug-running business had, a couple of years back, bought and sold some of those houses in a money-laundering scheme. They had, alas for them, been caught at it. More off-islanders run afoul of Vineyard law.

I slowed and shifted into four-wheel drive, then pulled onto the beach and headed east. Winter storms had worn the sands away but spring tides had returned them, so I could drive outside the dunes. With the waves slapping the beach on my right, I followed the truck tracks, watching the sky brighten over Chappaquiddick and taking note of the lights on Nantucket off to the south and east. Someday I'd have to go over there and have a look at that other island. But I'd been saying that for thirty years, ever since my father first took me to Wasque when I was five, and I hadn't done it yet. I was really thinking about bluefish anyway, not Nantucket.

A year ago I'd lucked out. On May fifteenth I'd fetched Wasque Point just as the blues had arrived for the season. All alone, I'd taken two dozen before sticking the rod in the spike and taking a coffee break. By the time George Martin and his fishing pal Jim Norris had arrived, I had forty-three fish and the school was gone. What could be more rewarding?

"You're just in time for the funeral," I'd said.

George and Jim had eyed my overflowing fishbox, then had fished all the way up East Beach and back while I stayed and admired the sunrise. When they got back, I was still on Wasque, drinking coffee.

"If you guys need a fish, help yourselves," I said.

"God is a giant bluefish, you know," said George, looking at my fish again. "You'll catch hell for this when you get to heaven. You have any more coffee in that jug?"

"You'd think a guy with as much money as you have would have his own coffee," I said as I poured.

"We had some," said Jim, "but it didn't last that whole trip up the beach and back."

"If you want to make your coffee last," I explained, "you have to spend some of your time catching fish. You see, when you're catching fish you don't have time to drink so much coffee. On the other hand, when you just ride around and drink coffee, you don't catch any fish, and by and by you not only don't have any fish but you don't have any coffee either. You understand what I'm saying?"

"I don't think I can stand this any more," said George. "Don't you have to go to work, Jim?"

"As a matter of fact, I do." Jim grinned. "Just in time, too. See you later, J.W."

George snagged a fish from my box. "I will take one of these. I promised Susie I'd bring her one for supper."

They drove off, and after a bit I followed. Back in Edgartown I got a good price for the fish because they were the first of the season.

That summer there had been a lot of blues around. So far this year, there weren't any. Maybe I'd be lucky again and meet them when they came in. But if so, I wasn't going to have Wasque to myself this time. There were fresh tire tracks ahead of me.

Wasque Point is on the southeast corner of Chappaquid-dick, the sometime island that is generally hooked to the Vineyard by a spit of sand running west along South Beach. When the sea breaks through the sandspit, Chappy is an island and the broken beach becomes Norton's Point; the rest of the time, Chappy is a peninsula. Wasque is one of the world's great bluefishing spots, thanks to the rip at its point which tosses bait up and about and attracts the voracious blues. Usually they arrived in May, but here it was early June and they were still on vacation. Had they no sense of duty?

My headlights pulled me along as the sky brightened, and sure enough there was a four-by-four parked in my favorite spot. It was two hours before the end of the west tide. Perfect timing. If the wily blues were coming, they should be coming now. I swung in beside the four-by-four and doused my lights. Dark against the brightening water, a lone fisherman, shapeless in waders and hooded sweat-shirt, was making his casts.

I looked at the four-by-four. It was unfamiliar. I knew most of the regulars and their vehicles. I looked at the sand near the four-by-four and saw no sign of fish lying there. I looked back at the fisherman and watched him reel in, set, and make his cast. The plug went away into the darkness. I looked out to sea but saw no splash of white indicating where the lure had landed. I got out, opened the back, and got out my Gra-lites. The air was nippy. I climbed into the waders, got my rod off the roof rack, and snapped a three-ounce Roberts onto the leader.

In the brightening air things were taking clearer shape. I looked again at the sand near the strange four-by-four but still saw no fish. Good. I looked at the fisherman. He was casting short and to the right. Just to make sure, I watched two more casts. Both went short and to the right. A starboard swinger, a familiar type among surfcasting tyros. I walked down on his left as he reeled in. The safe side. Supposedly. As I set to make my cast, a weight glanced off my head, snatched my cap, and flew down the beach into the surf. I felt the whip of fishline on my face and knew exactly what had happened; the fisherman, trying to straighten out his starboard cast, had overcom-pensated and made a radical cast to the left. My timing, impeccable as always, resulted in my head being in pre-cisely the right spot to be whacked by the plug.

"Hey!" I said.

"Jees!" said the fisherman.

"No damage," I said, disengaging myself from the line. "Now reel in. And when you get that hat back on the beach, ease off and let me get it unhooked. That's a valuable hat. It's got my shellfish license pinned to it."

The fisherman reeled, and the hat slid out of the surf and up onto the beach. It stopped at my feet. "It's the best thing I've landed so far," she said.

She said? Yes. She was a she. A fisherperson.

I unhooked my cap. It was almost new, one of those with an adjustable plastic strap on the back that says Caterpillar on the front. It was soaked and sandy. I shook it out, rinsed it in the surf, wrung it out, and put it on.

"I'm sorry," said the fisherperson, "but I came down here early just so I could practice without bothering anybody. Why did you have to stand so close? You could have any other place on the beach. Couldn't you see that I don't know what I'm doing?"

She was right. It was my own fault. "You're right," I said, "it's my own fault. It's just that you're standing right where I caught the first bluefish of the season last year."

"Well, there don't seem to be any here this morning."

She was hard to make out inside her sweatshirt and waders, but I had hopes of actually seeing her eventually because the light was getting brighter. Beyond her, coming from Katama, headlights were bouncing toward us. Another early riser.

"Don't give up on the fish yet," I said. "Look, do you really want to fish? If you do, you need a little help. It's okay to throw your plug every which way when you're alone, but once the blues come in, you won't be alone very often. The regulars will be lined up here shoulder to shoulder sometimes, and they'll not take kindly to having their lines crossed and getting plugs in their ears."

"Go ahead." She gritted her teeth. "Say something nasty about women trying to fish."

"Don't get testy," I said. "Everybody starts off the same way. There are a couple of tricks to this game just like any other one. I think you can get a kink or two out of your cast, if you want to. If you just want to be mad, go ahead. We're going to have company in about five minutes and then you'll be outnumbered and I won't have to be scared of you any more."

She glanced west toward the oncoming lights. When she turned back, I could see her face in the rising eastern light. Her mouth looked fairly set.

"Look," I said, "I'm not making a pass. I only go for gorgeous women, and right now you look like five pounds of shit poured into a ten-pound bag. Do you want a lesson or not?"

"Well, Jesus Christ!" she choked out. And then she began to laugh. A real belly laugh. After a bit she took a deep breath and nodded. "Yeah, sure. Why not? All of my conquests do my bidding. Show me how to cast. I'm sick of never knowing where this damned plug is going."

"It's hard in the dark," I said. "You should practice in the daylight so you can see where you're throwing. You want to see the splash where your plug hits the water, so you can make corrections. It's light enough now, if you know where to look." She had an ounce-and-a-half popper on her leader. Too light to throw well against the southwest wind. "You got a tacklebox?"

"In the Jeep. The guy at the tackle shop told me what to buy."

I got one of Spoff's guided missiles out of her box and put it on in place of the popper. "This is a good plug. It casts well and it catches fish, too."

I gave a demonstration. "Don't throw hard at first;

concentrate on throwing straight. See that light out there? That's a light buoy. Throw at that whenever you fish this spot and you'll be casting pretty straight out." I made a short cast. My Roberts splashed white and I reeled it in. "Now to begin with, make your casts right over your shoulder, not sidearm. That'll keep your plug from flying off in different directions. Bring your rod straight back and then swing it straight over. Release your line at, say thirty degrees above the horizon. Throw easy at first, because you're only trying for direction, not distance. Have you thrown your bail?"

"I'm not so dumb that I don't know enough to throw my bail!"

"How should I know how dumb you are? Besides, the ocean floor out there is covered with plugs snapped off of rods because the bail wasn't thrown. Several of them are mine. Okay, make sure your line isn't wrapped around the tip of your rod. That's it. Make your cast."

Her plug flew up in the air and landed about thirty feet from shore. She reeled in.

"Good," I said. "You're right on line, but you released a touch too soon. Try again."

She did, and the plug landed a bit farther out. She reeled in.

"Good. One more thing. Is the drag on your reel set right?"

"I don't know."

We traded rods and I showed her how to adjust the drag. "You want the line to run before it breaks, but not run too easily. There, that's about it." I got my rod back and watched her make two more casts. She threw straight. Not far, but straight. I turned away.

"Is that the end of the lesson?"

"That's it. I'm not a schoolteacher. The rest is practice. I came down here to fish."

I made my cast and dimly saw the splash of white out near the waves of the rip. No giant bluefish took it. No nice seven-pounder took it. Nothing took it. Beside me, the fisherperson made her casts. Short and straight. Nothing took her plug either.

On my fifth cast, George Martin's Wagoneer pulled up. He got out and leaned back against his door and watched me not catch a fish on two more tries. I walked up to see him. The fisherperson kept casting.

"You don't hook 'em up here," said George, "you catch 'em down there." He pointed to the fisherperson with his coffee cup. "How long has Zee been here?"

I followed his gaze. "She was here when I got here. Zee who?"

"Zee Madieras. She's a nurse up at the hospital. I didn't know she fished."

"She just started," I said. I leaned down and looked into the Wagoneer. George's daughter was there. "Well, well. Susie, what are you doing here? When I was your age, it was considered normal to sleep till noon."

Susie was sweet sixteen or so. A nice kid. Not too happy right now, though.

"Hi, J.W.," she said.

"What's up, kid? People pay thousands of dollars for the privilege of coming down to the Vineyard just so they can fish on Wasque, and here you are on the hallowed sand itself and your face is a mile long."

Sue sniffed and turned away. George touched my arm with his coffee cup and we walked to the back of his Jeep.

"I take it that I've been about as diplomatic as usual," I said.

"It's Jim Norris. He's decided to head back out west again. Just decided out of the blue. Leaving this afternoon, in fact."

"Kind of sudden. You two have been fishing together for over a year. I thought that he was on the island to stay. Good carpenter, good job, good guy . . ." My sentence trailed off into the air.

"Been like a son to me," said George. "Something else to Susie, it seems. Billy, too. The three of them got along fine these past months. It never occurred to me that it would end so quick." He glanced into the Wagoneer. "She's taking it pretty hard, Jeff. To tell you the truth, so am I. I was kind of hoping that Jim and Susie might make a go of it. He's quite a bit older, of course, but— Well, hell, I guess not."

I looked for something safe to say. "Surprised he didn't come out with you this morning to have a last go at the blues."

"Oh, he's going to have a go at them all right, but not off the beach. He and Billy are taking the *Nellie Grey* out this morning. Billy's idea. Sort of a going-away present. Susie wasn't invited. I guess the boys wanted to do something together before Jim takes off. We're all having lunch together afterward." He took his waders out of the back of the Wagoneer and climbed into them. "I figure that Susie and I will make a couple of casts here, then maybe drift up to Cape Pogue and watch the boys bring the boat out. Give Susie something to do." He took his rod off the roof rack and tapped on the Jeep window. "Hey, are we gonna fish or not, Susie? You have to get out of the car to catch 'em, you know."

Just as I was thinking how glad I was not to be sixteen and losing my first love again, the fisherperson down at the shore gave a shout. I looked and saw her rod bend.

"Good grief! She's on!"

I ran down and made my cast. I heard her reel singing.

"Help!" she shouted. "I'm reeling as fast as I can and my line's running out anyway! What do I do now?"

"Tighten your drag some more!"

"I can't! I don't have enough hands!"

Just then I felt a fish hit my plug. My rod bent and I set the hook. The fisherperson's line ran out and out. Christ! A moral dilemma. To bring in my own fish (the first of the season!) or help her save hers? Why hadn't I set her drag just a snippet harder? Curses! I ran sideways toward her. "Give me your rod and you take mine! Quick . . . That's it. . . ."

"My God, it feels like there's a whale out there!"

"Don't do anything but keep the line taut! Just do that!" I tightened her drag a bit more and then some more, carefully. She had a nice fish out there. The reel stopped singing and I took a few turns. "Look, here's what you do. Lift the tip of the rod toward you. No, get the butt between your legs first. That's it. Now lift the tip, and when you get it up, reel down like this." I hauled back and reeled down. "Let the rod work for you. That's it, that's it. Now, we change rods again . . ."

"Oops! Oh, my gosh!" My rod suddenly straightened and my line went slack. The fisherperson looked abashed.

Blast and drat! "He's off," I said. "Here, take your rod and land this one!" She ducked under my arm and I gave her her rod. It was nicely bent. She began to heave back and reel down. I moved away and reeled in my slack line. Everything was gone—fish, lure, and leader.

While I rigged up again, the fisherperson landed the first bluefish of the season. George got the second. Susie got the third.

I was fourth.

So it goes. Still, I found it interesting that I didn't feel as bad as I thought I should. I wondered why. It seemed out of character.

* 2 *

An hour later the fish were gone and the four of us were drinking coffee. In the warming morning Zee Madieras had doffed her hooded sweatshirt and no longer looked like five pounds of shit.

"My gosh—" She was laughing. "I never had so much fun! I'm exhausted! My arms feel like they're going to fall off." She looked at the sunlight dancing on the sea and at the empty beach curling away around the point. "You know, this is just astonishing. I'll bet that only three or four people out of every hundred who come down to the Vineyard ever get to a place like this or even think of fishing. All they know about is the beaches they can get to from the highways, the restaurants and the bars and the sailboats. How did I ever live this long without a four-wheel-drive vehicle?"

"It's a secret," George said, grinning. "Don't tell anybody. We want them to stay away." He rubbed his shoulder. "I've got an ache or two myself. Every year it takes me a week or so to get back into fishing shape."

She tapped him on the chest with her finger. "How about that ticker, George. Does your doctor know you do this stuff?"

He laughed. "If I go, this is how I want to go. I like to think that those heart attacks were God's way of telling me to give up work and get to fishing and hunting. It's been five years since I sold the company and came down here, and the old pump hasn't missed a beat." He tapped his shirt pocket. "I carry my nitro pills to keep everybody happy, though."

"I thought my own heart was going to burst when I was trying to land that first fish," said Zee. "It is really beautiful down here."

"Missed the green flash again," said Susie. "The magic moment went by during the blitz."

"What's the green flash?" asked Zee.

"They say that when the atmospheric conditions are just right at dawn or dusk, there's a flash of green just as the sun is touching the sea. I've never seen it."

"Don't look at me," I said. "I've never seen it either."

"Why do you cut the fish's throats when you land them?"

"I think it makes the meat taste better."

"Fishing lore," said George. "Everybody's got a different idea about how to do things."

Zee began counting fish. "Wow! What'll we do with them all? I never saw so many fish!"

"First, you get bragging rights," said Susie. "Look, here come some late arrivals. They'll see these fish and say something like 'They still around?' or 'When did they come in?' And then you get to say, 'You're just in time for the funeral.' "

From the west came two Jeeps.

"You get to say it, Zee," said George.

"Just act natural," I said. "Take a couple and toss them into George's fishbox just as they drive up. Then say it."

The first Jeep pulled up and the occupants surveyed the scene. Zee tossed a couple of fish into George's box and gave them a dazzling smile.

"They still around?" came the inquiry.

"You're just in time for the funeral," said Zee.

"They hit about an hour and a half before the end of the west tide," said Susie. Fishing lore.

Zee picked up two more fish. "Yeah, about then," she said and tossed the fish into the box.

The second Jeep pulled up. "Looks like they're here," said the driver.

"They were here," said the driver of the first Jeep.

"You mean . . ."

"Yep. You're just in time for the funeral."

Everyone laughed. "God," said the second driver, "how I love to say that and how I hate to hear it."

George looked at his watch. "Well, what do you say, Susie, shall we drift up to the lighthouse? The boys ought to be coming out in the boat about the time we get up there. We can make a couple of casts along the way, if you want."

We divied up the fish while the newcomers tried in vain for more. Zee had no fishbox, so without asking I tossed hers into my box. She looked at me. "You ever been up to the Cape Pogue light?" I asked. She shook her head. "Well, what do you say we trail George and Susie up there? It's a pretty drive. After we watch Billy and Jim come out, we'll come back down here, and you can pick up your four-by-four and follow me to the fish market. Then you can take your share of the loot and buy yourself a fish box of your very own so you won't be dependent on awkward but well-meaning strangers."

Zee looked at me. George and Susie looked at both of us.

"Hmmph," said George. He and his daughter got into his Wagoneer and headed up the beach.

"Well," I said, "what'll it be? You do have a choice. If you don't want to go up to Cape Pogue, I'll put my fishbox in your Jeep and you can take the catch to the market and give me my share of the money later."

"I don't even know how many fish I caught. I lost track after about the third one." She had a laugh that came from deep down, like bronze bells. "How many did you get?"

Fifteen. I always know. "I don't know," I said. "It's hard to keep track."

"How will we split the money, then?"

"Fifty-fifty is okay by me."

"You're a cheerful liar," she said. "You know exactly how many fish you caught." How did she know? "Okay, I'll go up to Cape Pogue with you. But I do have to get back before too long. I didn't get off work until two this morning, and I'm pretty wiped out."

"The first thing about riding around in waders is that it's hard to sit down in them," I said. "You can either take them off, which is not a good idea if we happen to find some fish because then you'll have to climb into them again, or you can loosen the suspenders and slide the waders down a bit so you can bend your knees."

"What do you suggest?"

"I suggest that you take them off. We've got all the fish we need, and I'd like to know what's really inside that ten-pound bag."

"If mine's a ten-pounder, yours is a twenty-pounder!"

"Flatterer!"

She had a great laugh, but she only loosened her shoulder straps before we chugged off north toward Cape Pogue. It was small-talk time.

"What are you looking at, out there in the water?" The sun was glancing off the water and I was squinting into the glare.

"Sometimes you can see fish."

"See fish? Under water?" She shaded her eyes against the dancing sunlight.

"Not now. There's nothing there. But when you drive along like this you can see them sometimes. There's a difference in the way the water looks when there's a school of bluefish moving along. If you cast into that water you can pick one up. Sometimes you'll see four-by-fours driving along and guys jumping out and casting a couple of times and then jumping back into the truck and driving on and jumping out again and casting. They're following the fish."

We were driving up East Beach, a beautiful stretch of sand where only fishermen can normally be found. It was lonely and lovely in the early morning sun. Far ahead, George's Wagoneer was a small dot on the empty sand.

"Why do they call you 'Zee'? An initial?"

"Short for Zeolinda. Named for my grandmother. She was from the Azores. How long you known George?"

"About five years. Just after we both came down here to stay. We met on the beach, fishing. He could really cast. Better than me, then, and probably still better."

"But can't you throw your plug out farther? I mean he's so much littler than you are. . . ."

"Some of the best casters are little guys sixty or seventy years old. They've got the right gear and the right technique and that beats size and strength every time. You're not very big, but the day may come when you're casting with the best of them."

"Really?"

"Really, if you practice."

Ahead, George stopped at a little point of sand and made a few casts. No action. He drove on and we followed.

"Why don't we try?" asked Zee.

"We'll try if you want to, but . . ."

"But if there were any fish there, George would have got one."

"Probably. The tide's slack now. Fishing will be better when it starts to run again. How did you meet George?"

"I met him in the hospital." She hesitated. "Do you know about his son, Billy?"

"I heard the rumors. That he was strung out on drugs, but took the cure. That he's clean now."

"Well, I met George and his family during all that. Billy was in Emergency before they flew him to the mainland for the cure. It wasn't a week later when I saw that article about George in *Time*. Did you see it?"

"The rags to riches to rags story? Millionaire entrepreneur leaves fast track for jeep and fishing rod and the simple life on Martha's Vineyard? Everybody on the beach read it. George took a lot of razzing from the regulars. They accused him of slumming."

"And what did he say to that?"

"He took it. And nobody ever mentioned it again. On the beach, it doesn't make any difference whether you wash dishes or own General Motors. They only care if you can cast straight and can kid around."

"Manly society."

"Mostly. There are half a dozen women, maybe, who belong, as it were. They have to meet the same tests."

We drove all the way up to the jetties. Shimmering waves, pale blue sky, gentle wind. A Chamber of Commerce day. Ahead of us stood the Cape Pogue lighthouse.

I stopped the Landcruiser and climbed out of my Gra-lites. Zee also shed her waders and we stashed both pair in the back.

"Guess what you don't look like any more," I said.

"Gosh, mister, you really know how to sweet-talk a lady. Do you really mean it?"

"Us Jacksons are noted for our silver tongues."

We drove toward the lighthouse. "What shall I call you, Mr. Jackson?"

"You can call me 'Jackson' or 'J.W.' or 'Jeff' or none of the above."

"Is that 'Geoff' with a G or 'Jeff' with a J?"

"It's J as in Jefferson."

"Don't tell me what the W stands for. Did your mother have a thing about presidents, or what?"

"She never explained."

"Does anybody ever call you 'Wash'?"

"No one living."

We hooked left off the beach just before the lighthouse and drove through the seagull nesting grounds up to the tower. George's Wagoneer was parked there. You could see Cape Cod fading off toward Chatham across the Sound, and the Oak Bluffs bluffs to the northwest. Beneath us, the cliff fell down to the beach, where jeep tracks formed a sandy road. It's one of my favorite spots. Someday when I win the lottery I may buy one of the lonely houses out there.

"How do these people get supplies?"

"By four-by-four or by boat. There's Edgartown, over to the west. By water it's not too far. By car, the way we've just come, it's a long haul. This is the place for people who like to be alone."

"Do you like to be alone?"

I thought about it. "I'm alone whether I like it or not." She gave me a long look.

George had his binoculars out and was looking toward Edgartown, trying to spot the *Nellie Grey* coming out. She was his boat, a nice thirty-foot fishing toy for the man who could afford such toys. She had clean lines and a wide cockpit with three chairs for trolling. She was the kind of boat I'd want if I didn't prefer sail.

From the north I saw another boat coming. A long black expensive job with outriggers and a pulpit, the sort of boat you could take a long way out with no trouble at all. She was on a course that would take her a half-mile or so east of us. I guessed she was on her way to the swordfishing grounds south of Nomans or maybe even farther. She was not the sort of boat that hung on the Wasque rip trolling for bluefish. I thought maybe I'd seen her in the Oak Bluffs harbor or in Vineyard Haven, but I wasn't sure.

Beyond her, other boats were coming out. How did they know the bluefish had arrived?

"There she is," said George, looking through his glasses. "I hope they don't have any more trouble with that engine."

"Don't worry, Daddy," said Susie, "the yard checked it out and I did, too. I took her out yesterday afternoon and everything was fine."

I must have had a question mark on my face.

"Gas leak," said Susie. "One of the lines in the engine compartment. You could smell the fumes sometimes, so we took it in. Just a bad connection, but out of the way so it was tricky to find. But they found it and fixed it, and yesterday I took *Nellie* halfway to Falmouth and back. No problem."

Now the *Nellie Grey* was in sight, moving smoothly out

with mild following waves, the wind at her back. She came past the lighthouse and we could see Jim and Billy. They waved and we waved back, and they went on out beyond the shallows that reach east from Cape Pogue. Beyond the *Nellie Grey* the long black boat altered her course to hold outside the *Nellie*'s turn as she swung south beyond the shallows to follow the beach toward Wasque.

"Come on," said George, lowering his binoculars, "let's go back to Wasque so we can watch them fish the rip. The east tide will be running and there may be something there."

Susie, looking sad, nodded and turned to the Wagoneer.

"We'll follow you down," I said, "but then we're going on into town. We want to sell these fish."

"And I've got to get some sleep," said Zee. "I've got duty again tonight, and right now I'm frazzled out."

Just at that moment the *Nellie Grey* exploded. A great red and yellow flower opened from the sea and expanded into the air. Petals of flame and stalks of debris shot up and arched away as a ball of smoke billowed from the spot where the *Nellie* had been. A moment later the boom of the explosion hit us, and the sea around the *Nellie* was one of flame. I thought I saw a body arc into the burning water.

The black boat turned and I could see her white bow wave as she sped in toward the burning wreckage. I thought I could see a figure thrashing in the oily water. The black boat came in, dangerously close, and someone leaned over the side and dragged a man up over the rail.

Behind me I heard a cry and turned to see Susie with her father in her arms. His hand was groping toward his shirt pocket as his knees buckled.

Then Zee was beside him, helping him with his nitroglycerin pills and I was on the C.B. radioing the Chappy beach patrol to alert the Emergency Center that we were coming in with a heart-attack patient and to tell the harbormaster and Coast Guard that the *Nellie Grey* had just blown up off the Cape Pogue light.

* 3 *

We took the Wagoneer because it was bigger and more comfortable, and I drove us south along Cape Pogue Pond. I cut over the Dike Bridge and raced to the ferry. On the far side the ambulance waited. The ambulance took George and Susie and Zee and went off, sirens wailing. The tourists stared. Beyond the Edgartown light the harbor patrol was roaring out toward Cape Pogue.

I took George's Wagoneer out to his house. Nobody home. His wife had gone to the hospital. It had been a bad day for the Martins. I left the keys with the housekeeper and hitched back into town.

I got my dinghy at Collins Beach and went putt-putting off to Cape Pogue Pond, where I beached the boat and walked up to the lighthouse to get the Landcruiser. Out in the sound there were boats hovering around the spot where the *Nellie Grey* had gone down. The Coast Guard and the Edgartown harbormaster's boat were there, and I could see skin divers in the water. I remembered Marcus Aurelius's advice: Do not act as if thou were going to live ten thousand years. Death hangs over thee.

The fish in my box—mine and Zee's—were too soft to keep, so I tossed them off the cliff and watched the seagulls swoop in for the feast. The morning that had started off so beautifully had turned all sour. I drove back, picked up the dinghy, and went down to Wasque. The terns and gulls fed along the edge of the water, and I saw oyster catchers and a little blue heron. Nothing had changed for them; the sun still showered light down upon the sand and sea. The wind still blew softly from the southwest. The sky was still pale blue. At Wasque a dozen four-by-fours were lined up, and poles were bending in the hands of fishermen as the east tide ran. I heard shouts and laughter as the fish were reeled in. I drove on by.

The next day I read all about it in the *Gazette*. George was still alive and was expected to recover. Billy was alive, though burned by both the explosion and his efforts to save Jim Norris. Jim was dead, his body having been recovered from the wreck by skin divers. Billy had been saved by the quick action of the captain of the *Bluefin*, which had picked him up and raced with him to Oak Bluffs, radioing ahead for an ambulance to meet them at the docks.

Credit was given to nurse Zeolinda Madieras, who had accompanied George to the hospital. Tim Mello, skipper of the *Bluefin*, was praised by the boat's owner, Fred Sylvia, by the passengers aboard the *Bluefin*, and by his mother. About Jim Norris there was little. He was from Oregon, his parents had been notified. He was well remembered by those who knew him as a pleasant, hard-working man who enjoyed outdoor work and fishing. A tragic loss.

I wrote a note to George accusing him of being too rotten to die and saying I'd see him after he was no longer news. I told him my fish had gone soft because of him and that the next time we'd haul him in in my Landcruiser and leave his Wagoneer out there so *his* fish could spoil.

Then I went out and hoed my garden for a while. I

plant early in April, and greenies were appearing in little rows. I'd have radishes and lettuce any day now, and my beans and peas looked good. I wondered if my carrots would be as bad as usual and if I'd been right to try broc and cauliflower again since I'd never yet managed to make them grow.

I had rows of flowers planted between the rows of vegetables, but had a hard time telling which little plants were flowers and which were weeds. I'm better at recognizing vegetables than flowers.

I was through hoeing and had the sprinkler turned on, and was having a beer as a reward for my hard work when a car came down my driveway.

Since I live in the woods at the end of a narrow, bumpy road, I don't see many people in my yard who don't want to be there. I don't get many in any case.

The car stopped and Susie Martin got out. I was glad I was at least wearing shorts. Sometimes I'm inclined to walk around my place wearing only sandals. I have tender, flat feet.

"Hey, kid," I said, "how's the old man?"

She had an odd look about her. "He's okay. I guess it wasn't too bad. Learning that Billy was okay helped a lot."

"How's Billy?"

"He's okay." She had a way with words. "I want to talk with you, J.W."

She was serious and nervous.

"Sure, kid. Sit down. Want a Coke?" This was the first time she'd ever been to my place, and she was looking it over in a halfhearted way. "Old hunting camp," I said. "My father bought it way back when island land was cheap. I inherited it."

"Daddy says you were a policeman once."

"Not anymore. Now I'm just a guy on a medical pension."

She wandered to one of the almost-matched lawn chairs I'd salvaged from the Edgartown dump and had repainted until they looked almost new. I sat down in the one I'd just gotten up from. She ran her fingers over the chair's plastic webbing. She was wearing shorts and one of those shirts with an animal above the left pocket. Restrained yet expensive, stylish in the Martha's Vineyard summer mode. My shorts were from the thrift shop. It's the way I like to live.

"I don't know how to say what I want to say. . . ."

I got up. "Sit down. I'll get you a drink."

I went inside and got a Coke from the fridge for her and another Molson for myself. I skimp on what I can, but one cannot skimp on one's beer. Except toward the end of the month. I gave her the can and watched her diddle with it, then take a sip. I sat down and had a snort myself.

"You're going to think I'm a nut . . ."

"Take a chance."

She gripped the can with both hands and looked right at me. "That wasn't an accident. Somebody tried to kill my brother! I checked the *Nellie Grey* out the day before it blew up. There wasn't a thing wrong with it. Somebody did something to it before Billy and Jim went out that morning!" She twisted the can in her hands. "Poor Jim. They didn't care about him. All they wanted was Billy!"

"Who wanted him? Why?"

She was fierce. "Who do you think? Billy's druggie friends, of course! They're afraid he'll turn them in now that he's gotten straight!"

Melodrama. Did I roll my eyes? I saw her looking at me with that furious expression youth wears when it's speaking seriously and is taken lightly. She leaped to her feet.

"Sit."

She sat, eyes aflame. I sucked down some more beer. "Don't get put off. It's my face. I play roles with it. I look the way I feel or sometimes I look the way I think I'm supposed to feel or the way I think I should pretend to feel. That's probably why I never made detective. You got to admit your story sounds like television: 'My brother's gone straight, and the mob is afraid he'll talk.' "

"Why do you say 'got to'? You know better!"

True. "Sorry. It's more game playing. Probably a bad habit. No more games, okay? Now, who's after Billy? Why? How do you know?"

She leaned forward. A nice young womanish body. If there was a God, some lucky fellow would one day benefit from it. But not middle-aged me. "I don't have to tell you, do I, that this island isn't just a happy summer resort, but that there's a big drug trade here, too. You know that this place may be the drug capital of the East Coast. You know how easy it is for expensive boats and planes to come and go from this island without attracting any attention at all, and you know that every year or so they have a big drug bust involving people or houses down here for laundering money or other stuff like that.

"My brother was very strung out for years right here on this island, and he knows that scene. It almost killed him, but now he's going straight. He's at Brown, you know. He's not dumb. He's on the dean's list! But I saw him in Oak Bluffs last week, just outside the Fireside. Jim was with him. I saw one of the creeps he used to know shove Billy, and I ran over just as Jim stepped between them. But I heard the guy say, 'You'll get yours!' before he ran off. I know a dopehead when I see one, and he was a dopehead. It was that Danny Sylvia, damn him! Damn him!"

"You know him?"

"I know him, all right. He's the one who got Billy started. At the tennis club, would you believe it! Mom and Mrs. Sylvia played there and the next thing you know that damned Danny had Billy using first one thing, then the next. I hate him! I hate her!"

"Her?"

"His mother!" Susie's face was hard and sullen. "She brought Danny there. She got him and Billy together. They played tennis. My mother never liked it."

I emptied my Molsons. "What do you mean? Never liked what?"

Susie was suddenly evasive, the way people are when they believe something that's unpleasant and hard to know for sure. "Mom just stopped playing tennis with Maria Sylvia, that's all. I don't know why. Ask her!" She stared down at her Coke.

I thought that she did know why. "What about Billy and Danny?"

"The Sylvias sent dear Danny off to take the cure, I heard." Her lip curled. "By that time, of course, Billy was hooked!"

"But he got unhooked." I thought of something. "Maybe your mother blamed Danny's mother for what Danny did to Billy, just like you do."

"Maybe." Maybe not. She sensed my doubt. "You think I'm not telling you what I think, don't you?"

Everyone lies when he thinks it's important. "It would help, maybe, if I knew what you think."

"No." She shook her head back and forth. "If you want

to know why my mother broke off from Danny's mother, you can find out from her. I want you to find out who it was who tried to kill my brother, that's all! Find out who killed Jim! I know it was that Danny Sylvia! I want you to get him!" And then suddenly she was crying. Great chest-heaving sobs. I climbed out of my chair and went over to her. She shook my hand from her shoulder and sobbed some more. I went into the house and got another beer. When I came out, she was walking to her car. "I knew you wouldn't," she said in a voice like broken ice. "First the police wouldn't and now you won't. I knew it!"

"You're wrong," I said. "I'll give it a try. I'll let you know."

She drove away, and I finished my beer.

* 4 *

I went down to Harborside Marine, where the manager met me with less than enthusiasm. He was wearing a clean shirt. His name was Joe Snyder. We'd had a go-around a few years back when his outfit had charged me $104 to replace a condenser in my outboard. As a result I'd learned to repair my own outboard and only went to Harborside Marine for parts. Joe knew my opinion of his prices.

"I don't think I have to tell you anything," he said. "I've already talked to the cops and the Coast Guard and the Martins' lawyer. Your lawyer can talk to my lawyer."

"I don't have a lawyer," I said. "I just want to check a story. Martin's daughter says she took the *Nellie Grey* out the day before the explosion and that everything was fine. Did she do that?"

"Yeah. She went out for a couple of hours. The boat was fine. There wasn't ever much of a problem with it. A loose connection, that's all. I took the boat out myself before the Martin girl went out. There was nothing wrong with the boat. You a private investigator? You nosing around for the insurance company?"

"No and no. Where was the boat put when Susie Martin brought it back?"

29

"Right there at that dock. Why?"

"Was it refueled when she brought it in?"

"Yeah. We topped off the tank after she tied up, and there wasn't any fuel leak when we did it. Look, I'm busy . . ."

"Could anyone have gotten to the boat during the night?"

"We have a night watchman. He didn't report anything. What are—"

"Could anyone have gotten aboard from the water? Come along in a dinghy or maybe swimming?"

"Swimming? I suppose it's possible. But the boat was still locked tight the next morning when Martin and Norris took her out. If there'd been any sign of tampering, young Martin would have let me know about it. He never lets us forget that his old man is paying us a good penny for looking after the *Nellie*—" He corrected himself. "That is, he never let us forget it when the *Nellie* used to be here. . . ."

I doubted neither that George paid a pretty penny nor that Billy let Snyder remember it.

"Did Billy Martin act worried or say anything about any trouble he might be in?"

"No. He was pretty cheerful, as a matter of fact. He and Norris were heading for the Wasque rip to try for blues on the early east tide, and they told us they'd bring us some fish. What's all this about? Why these questions?"

"And the boat was fine when they went out?"

"Motor ran like silk. What's going on?"

"Thanks," I said and walked away. By not telling him what I was doing, I figured I got back about two cents of the $104 he'd charged me for the condenser. Revenge, as the Italians say, is a dish best eaten cold. If I refused ever to explain anything to Joe Snyder for the next several hundred years, I'd finally be even with him. Patience is important in such matters.

Edgartown is a beautiful village of brick sidewalks and white or weathered gray shingled houses. Along Water Street the whaling financiers built their great white houses, each seemingly more splendid than the next. There is old money aplenty, and the harbor is filled with millions of dollars' worth of power and sailing yachts in the summertime. It is a fashionable place to have a summer house, and the police force behaves accordingly. Of late a couple of bars have begun to disturb the evening quiet that was once so characteristic of the town, and the police have been increasingly obliged to haul noisy, mostly young drunks off to jail.

I went to the police station. Helen Viera was sitting at a desk wearing her white blouse and blue skirt. Her badge was golden, but not gold. Summer colors. The tourist season had arrived, Helen said, smiling. I could find the chief downtown somewhere.

There isn't much to downtown Edgartown, so he wasn't hard to find. He was at the four corners, where Main and Water streets cross, directing traffic. Beyond the parking lot at the foot of Main, tall sails were slanting out of the harbor against a northeast wind.

I told him what Susie had told me and what Joe Snyder had told me. He glanced at me without expression, then watched traffic go by for a while. Edgartown is mostly narrow one-way streets, and traffic was already heavy. I've always wondered why there are so many cars downtown when the weather is as nice as it was that day. Why aren't those people out at the beach or watching birds or something? The chief waved a hand and a young officer came and replaced him on traffic detail. A summer rent-a-cop. A Criminal Justice student at some New England college, no doubt.

"I know Billy Martin," he said. "Somebody on the island lost a good customer when he took the cure, but I don't know anybody who'd try to rub him out. Why should anybody do that?"

"The theory is that Billy is about to squeal on his old buddies. Danny Sylvia in particular."

"But Danny Sylvia's taken the cure, too, from what I hear, so what's Billy going to say that everybody doesn't already know—that a couple of years ago Danny might have been Billy's dealer. No news there. No reason for Danny to do Billy in. I'm afraid that Billy's sister may still be in shock or some such thing, you know what I mean?"

"Well, everybody says that the boat was running just fine, but it blew up for some reason or other. And Billy'd been into the dope scene, and some of those guys play rough. . . ."

He nodded, his eyes floating up and down the street like cops' eyes always do, even when they're just shooting the breeze. "There's a lot of dope around, all right. All kinds. You name it, we've got it. Back when people took marijuana seriously, there was a guy down here who called himself Johnny Potseed. He drove all over the island planting seeds for later public consumption. We knew who he was, but we never could catch him. Since then, the business has gotten a lot more sophisticated, and we don't catch most of the new operators either. We've got boats and planes coming in here all summer long. Big ones. Little ones. Yachts, fishing boats, you name it. We got movie stars and bigwigs of all kinds and big money. All kinds of money coming and going and just looking for something to buy. The narcs make a big bust every now and then, but mostly we spend our time on nickel-and-dimers. Look at the report of the court sessions that they print in the *Gazette*—it's almost two pages long, and half of it is possession arrests. When I first went to work for the town, there wasn't a half page devoted to court. All we had were a few drunk drivers. Times have changed, all right.

"The island police forces are straight out just taking care of the heart attacks, the moped accidents, the traffic, and the drunks. We don't have the manpower to stop the drugs even if the public wanted us to. But it's like prohibition, you know? There's a market for drugs, and where there's a market there's an organization that's going to service it." He allowed himself a faint snort of frustration. "Anyway, I still don't know of anybody who'd want to do in Billy Martin."

"You know any more about Danny Sylvia than you've told me?"

"I hear he went out to California last week. Summer school at UCLA, or something like that."

While I thought about that, a car stopped and the driver beckoned. The chief leaned toward the window, listened, told the woman driving that there wasn't any ferry to Block Island, and stepped back.

"It's amazing," he said. "I had a driver ask me where the bridge was to the mainland. Can you believe it? I'll be glad when Labor Day comes."

"What's the latest on the explosion? Any theories?"

"They're going to leave the boat where it is. Pretty expensive to bring it up, and not any real reason for it, from what I'm told. There's not enough left of the boat to be a navigation hazard. Jim Norris was dead when they got to him. Burned, and with pieces of gear blown into him and through him. Probably never knew what hit him. Everything says accident. Young Martin would probably have cashed in, too, but I guess he was up on the forward deck when everything went off. Blew him into the water. Anyway, I don't think the daughter has a case."

"Billy have any special pals in town? Anybody he hung around with when he was walking on the wild side?"

"No. Oak Bluffs was his stomping ground in those days. Edgartown was too quiet for bouncing Billy. If you insist on nosing around, you'll have to do it in O.B."

"Thanks," I said.

He said I was welcome.

I drove up past the state beach to Oak Bluffs. The road was lined with parked cars on the beach side. Between the cars and the blue waters of Vineyard Sound the beach was crowded with June People, intent on tanning. By the time the July People came down, the June People would be brown and feeling healthy. The July People would be self-conscious about their pallor and would work hard at what I call Browning the Meat so that the August People would, in their turn, feel as conspicuous as the July People once had. One advantage about vacationing in June is that everybody is pale and wan.

Circuit Avenue, Oak Bluff's main street, is a mixture of honky-tonky shops and bars. The Day People arrive there, take the sightseeing buses around the island, buy souvenirs and snacks, get back on the boat, and go home. Oak Bluffs does quite well by this business. There are several other sides of the town, though. The island hospital is there, there's some big money in big houses, the tabernacle is surrounded by wonderful gingerbread houses from Victorian camp meeting days, and the town is a major resort for well-to-do blacks, one of the few on the East Coast. I drove to the hospital.

George was in intensive care. As she went out, the nurse told me not to be long.

I sat down and looked around. "Where's Billy? I thought you two might be sharing a room."

"No, he's down the hall. He's got some bruises and he lost some hair and skin, but he's going to be fine, thank God. They're just keeping him under observation for a while. He should be out in a few days."

"I'll drop by and see him on my way out. He's had his troubles. First drugs and now this."

George grunted in the affirmative. "Well, he got loose from the dope and he's going to make it away from this, too. If I'd made him go to summer school, he'd be up at Brown now, instead of down here in the hospital. But you know how kids are. He wanted to be on the island for the summer. I only made him promise one thing—that he'd stay away from the Fireside. That's where his old buddies still hang out, and I didn't want him mixing with them again."

I wondered if Susie had told him what she'd told me: that just last week she'd seen her brother right outside the Fireside, having an argument with an old buddy. I guessed she hadn't.

"Shame about Jim," I said.

He nodded. "They say he never knew what hit him, probably. I'll miss him. He said he wasn't planning to come back this way again, once he got back out west. Funny, when I was a kid the phrase 'went west' meant died. Jim went west, all right. Too damned bad. He was a good guy. I cared about him."

"You've still got your son. And your daughter. And your health."

"I know. I have everything, really, and I still feel bad. I'll be out of here before long." He tapped his chest. "The old clock skipped a few ticks, but it's good for several more years. Lucky, though. Damned nitro pills didn't help. I'm gonna get some fresh ones. Good thing Zee was there, or I might not be able to feel anything. Still, I'm damned if I intend to lie down for the rest of my life just to avoid dying. I plan to be on the beach again as soon as they let me out of here."

The nurse walked in, smiled at him, and waved me out.

Down the hall I found Billy's room. Billy had bandages wrapped around one arm and more on his head. The hair that I could see was singed short. He'd had a longish beach-boy kind of haircut, but it would take a while to grow another one. He was about twenty, a kid with his father's features. Right now the features were covered with some sort of salve. His lips were split and he had singed eyelashes and brows.

"How you doing?" I sat down.

"I'm okay. What are you doing here?" He had reason to be surprised. We'd never been close. When I'd first met him he'd been strung out and snide, one of those users who think that their habit makes them superior to straight folk. I hadn't seen much of him since he'd taken the cure.

"I came to see your old man. He told me you were here. I want to ask you something I couldn't ask him."

"Sure. What? If it's about the accident, I'm afraid I can't tell you much. I don't know what happened."

"Tell me about that morning, before the explosion happened. Was there anything odd about the boat when you got aboard?"

"What do you mean?" He winced when he frowned.

"Your sister thinks somebody fixed it so the explosion would happen."

He paled beneath his burn, and his eyes widened like a deer's before a gun. "What? What do you mean? What are you . . ." His voice rose and thinned.

"Your sister thinks that somebody tried to blow you up and that it was to keep you from talking about your old drug buddies. She asked me to check it out."

"She's crazy. She's just crazy with worry. And shook up because of poor Jim." He paused. "She's wrong. I've been away from the drug scene for over a year. Since last summer. I don't see that crowd anymore."

"Somebody saw you last week in front of the Fireside. They say you and your friend Danny Sylvia got in an argument and that he said he'd get you."

"Who told you that?" He leaned up off the pillows, then eased back. "Of course. Susie told you. She got there about the time Danny said that. But believe me, it didn't mean anything. That's just Danny's way. Besides, Danny's not on dope anymore, either. He's straight, like me. Anyway, he left for California to go to summer school, so it couldn't have been him."

"What was the argument about, then?"

"A girl. It was about a girl we both know. You know what I mean?" He gave a small grin, then stopped it. It hurt for him to grin just like it hurt for him to frown.

"Was there anything odd or unusual about the boat that morning. Any sign of tampering, maybe?"

He thought. "No, nothing at all. The boat was locked

up, the tanks were full, everything was fine. Jim and I started her up and took her right out. No problems."

"Did you smell any gas fumes?"

"No. Well, maybe. But nothing that I thought anything about. Nothing at all, really. Just that sort of oily smell you get sometimes from an engine."

"We saw you and Jim as you passed the lighthouse. Then what happened?"

"We were rounding the shallows off Cape Pogue when I noticed that the anchor line was adrift off the foredeck. I left Jim at the helm and went forward. I was up there coiling line when it happened. I guess it blew me overboard. The next thing I knew I had a mouthful of water and all I could see was fire. I tried to see Jim, to get back to him, but . . ." His cracked lips tightened and he stared ahead of him, looking hard at a spot in midair.

"Okay, Billy. Don't think about that."

"I can't help thinking about it. I'll always think about it. I'll never forget it. Jim was my friend and I couldn't help him!"

I let a moment pass. When his eyes were again in focus on me, I said, "One more time, then—you're sure that nobody had any reason to want to get rid of you?"

He came back from his gloom and almost smiled. "Oh, I'm sure that some of my old pals wouldn't have shed any tears if it had been me that got killed out there. But none of them would actually do it, you know? They're just dopey people trying to find money for their next fix, they're not killers. Hell, they haven't got their shit together enough to be killers."

"There's a lot of dope on this island, and the guys who are running the show have a lot of money at stake. Their shit is plenty together."

He shook his head and grimaced. "I wouldn't know. I never knew any guys like that. I got my stuff from friends." He thought back. "Friends. Sure, some friends . . ."

I drove home. Sometimes people know things they don't know they know, so they can't tell you. Other times they know things they don't want to tell you. Other times they just lie. As I drove past the June People soaking up the rays of the Vineyard sun and splashing in the little waves hissing on the beach, I thought about the various things I'd been told.

When I got home, I opened a beer and made lunch. If you live alone you're apt to start eating carelessly, tossing down whatever comes easiest because it doesn't seem worthwhile spending time on food if there's no one to share it with. I try to treat myself like a guest. Today my guest got ham and cheese sandwiches and deli-style half-sour pickles with his beer. A feast fit for a king. Then I spent half an hour with the food processor, chopping veggies and mixing up a jug of gazpacho: into a gallon jar went tomato juice, chopped tomatoes, onions, cukes, green peppers, and garlic; and salt, pepper, oil, and sherry. I put the cap on the jar, shook everything up, and put it in the fridge. Tomorrow it would be delish, with or without vodka.

After I'd washed and stacked my cooking tools, I got the *Gazette* and found a story I'd glanced at earlier. A small story about an enigmatic ongoing investigation by the D.A. and off-island law enforcement people. The *Gazette* prefers to underemphasize the dark side of Vineyard doings, so not much was said, and it was not said deep in the paper. Or maybe not much was said because the reporter didn't know much. I reread the story of the explosion and noted again that Jim Norris's parents lived in Oregon. I'd never heard of the town.

I dug out my Boston phonebook. It was five years out of date, but it still had the number I wanted. It belonged to a reporter who works for the *Globe*. We'd met when I was a Boston cop, and we'd hit it off the way a cop and reporter sometimes will. He still owed me a favor, particularly since I'd had him down to the island a couple of times during the fall bluefish derby.

"Quinn, it's pay-up time."

"All right, I confess that it was me who robbed the Brinks truck in Plymouth, but I spent all the money on wild women, so all you can do is throw me in jail. How's the back?"

"Fine. Listen, I'm looking into something down here and I keep running into drugs. Everybody I talk to has something to say, but nobody is really saying anything. Is there something going down? Something here on the island? You've got a long nose; I figure you might have heard."

"Yeah, I've heard something. I've heard that you aren't a cop anymore. Not even a private one."

"Quinn, you remember that fourteen-pound blue you got last September? Well, you remember him good, because that was the last blue I'm ever going to put on your hook for you."

"No, no, not that. Anything but that." Quinn yawned. "Okay, I did hear something. The feds and the state are both in on it. DEA and all that, so their security has some holes in it. Not a sieve, just some holes. It'll be a good story. Giant drug bust in affluent summer resort. Big crooked money side by side with respectable old money. Famous names sharing their island with underworld kingpins. Balzac quoted once again to the effect that behind every great fortune lies a great crime. That sort of thing. Anyway, it's supposed to happen soon. I hear they've got infiltrators down there and maybe a stoolie or two. Just rumor, you know. The D.A. on the Cape is coordinating things, I'm told. That what you wanted to know?"

"That's part of it. Do you have any names?"

"No names yet. But I did hear that there was a Portuguese connection."

"Portugal Portuguese or the local variety?"

"I don't know. I'll dig around if you want."

"Dig around. Half the population down here is part Portuguese at least. Get a name for me."

I hung up and thought of one Portuguese name in particular: Zeolinda Madieras.

* 5 *

"This is my lucky day," said the chief. "Imagine, two conversations with you in a single twenty-four-hour period." This time he was in the patrol car outside the station. I'd been waiting for him.

I climbed in beside him. "A snow white dove has descended from heaven, circled three times around my head, landed on my shoulder, and whispered in my ear that there's a big drug bust about to come down hereabouts in the very near future. My dove says that the big narcs have little narcs inside the local operation and have lined up some stool pigeons, too. My dove says there may be a Portagee in the middle of it all. Now whoever that Portagee might be, he wouldn't maybe be worried about Billy Martin squealing, would he?"

"Gee, you talked a whole paragraph there," said the chief admiringly. "You're becoming verbal instead of maintaining the stoic calm I've come to expect from you. Where did you learn about those doves and all? In Sunday School?"

"It was part of the academy training program. We had to learn to talk to God before we talked to the sergeants. What about my boy Billy? Does he have a problem nobody wants to tell me about?"

"Like I told you, I can't think of any reasons why anybody would be mad at Billy. I can think of why somebody might be mad at you, though. Making wild talk like that about Portagees. You're not a Portagee, you know. Somebody might think you're prejudiced."

"Oh, dear me. Gosh and gee whiz. Who tells the Portagee jokes around here, anyway? Me? No, you do. And pretty bad ones, too."

"That's different. I'm a Portagee myself, so I can say anything I want to about them. You're some kind of off-islander without a drop of Portagee blood in you. You should only insult your own kind."

"I've lived on this island so long now that some Portagee has rubbed off on me. Besides, I insult everybody indiscriminately. What can you tell me about this action that's coming down?"

"I can tell you this—as far as you're concerned, nothing's happening. You hear me? Nothing's happening. My advice is to stay away from what you're nosing around in."

"You want me to stay away from whatever it is that's not happening, right?"

"You're sharp as a razor, J.W. That bullet might have clipped your gizzard, but it never touched your brain. I'm serious—stay away."

"If somebody's mad enough at Billy to try to blow him up in the *Nellie Grey*, the same somebody might be mad enough to try for him while he's in the hospital flat on his back."

"You watch too much TV. Nobody's after Billy."

"Who's the Portagee Connection?"

"I don't know what you're talking about. I hear the blues are in. Go fishing for a couple of weeks."

We both got out of the cruiser and looked at each other across the hood. "I don't own a TV," I said.

"You're fast with the repartee," said the chief enviously. Then his tone changed. "I don't want anything messing up this action. I don't want the bad guys getting any tipoff that there's an axe over their heads. It's happened in the past and we're trying to find the leak right now. The best thing you can do for me is to stay out of this until the dust settles."

"You think the leak's local? Remember, there are state and federal people involved, too, and they're not famous for keeping secrets. Hell, I heard about this from Boston."

"From a confidential source, no doubt."

"Of course."

"Well, your source didn't tell you when all this was going down, did he? That's the key that's still in the lock, and I don't want it out till it's time to make arrests. Twice in the past two years we've found empty space where we should have found people and evidence. Somebody's tipping them off."

"And nobody's after Billy, eh? It's a comfort to us average citizens to know that you men in blue are out there."

"Protect and serve," said the chief. "That's our motto." He walked into the station. Through the window I saw Helen Viera turn away and move back to her desk. She'd been watching us and probably wondering why the chief was parked out there talking when she probably had plenty of work for him to do at his desk.

I found the Landcruiser right where I'd left it, and got out my tide table. The end of the west tide was about seven o'clock. I found a phone booth and called the Martin house. George's wife, Marge, was home. She was doing housework, a woman's solution to being nervous, she said. I told her I'd seen George and Billy at the hospital and that they both looked pretty good, and I asked to talk to Susie. She was at the hospital. Marge thanked me for my help and I managed a reply in the "Aw, shucks, ma'am, it was nothin' " mode. I asked if I could come out and talk with her and she said yes, so I drove out.

I didn't know Marge Martin very well. George and I shared the fishing spots, but Marge was in the tennis and cocktails set, where my feet rarely trod. Still, we hit it off well enough. She, like George, was only lately rich. She hadn't been born to it and she remembered what it was like to have to work. If she wanted to play tennis and never break a nail digging clams, it was okay with me. Everybody to his own style, I say.

She met me at the door. She was fifty or so, tanned, in good shape from tennis. Her hair was short and fashionable and she was wearing summer shorts and a pastel top decorated in rich-girl pink and green. The parent-of-preppies look. Not bad.

She took my hands in hers. "Oh, J.W., I can't thank you enough. If it hadn't been for you and Zee Madieras . . ."

I there-there'd and smiled, and she smiled back and led me into their living room. It was an old New England house but with modern touches, which made it a lot more comfortable than it had been when the old New Englanders had been obliged to live in it. I liked it. We sat down and I got right to the point.

I told her about Susie coming to me and about what she'd said about everything, including Mrs. Sylvia and her son Danny. Emotions moved over Marge Martin's face, changing the way her skin fit over the bones beneath it. But the emotions were elusive to me. I asked her what she had to say about Susie's ideas.

She shook her head. "I can't believe that anybody would try to kill Billy. That's not possible. Billy's been away from drugs for over a year. He's no threat to anyone. He never was! I can't imagine where Susie got those ideas!"

"What about Danny Sylvia? Susie says he's the one who got Billy started on dope in the first place. She saw them a week ago, arguing. She says Danny threatened him."

She put her hands on her knees. "No, I can't imagine it. Maria and Fred Sylvia were just as horrified as I was when they learned that Danny was using drugs. They sent him off to some place in California for the cure. I remember how furious and determined they were, how they forced Danny into the toughest program they could find and made him stay there until he was absolutely freed from his addiction. I don't think that Danny would dare get involved with drugs again. He's in college out west somewhere, I think. No, I can't imagine Danny being so angry with Billy that he'd threaten him. Susie must have been mistaken."

"Why did you stop playing tennis with Maria Sylvia?"

She looked at me with secret eyes.

I gave her a suggestion. "Was it because her son had corrupted yours?"

She tossed her head in a peculiarly youthful way, which allowed me to glimpse her daughter in her. "No. If you want to know the truth, it was because she likes young men too much. She's my age, but she surrounds herself with men half her age, with boys young enough to be her sons. She has one of them working in her house who doesn't do anything but drive her around or play tennis with her.

He's supposed to be her husband's bodyguard, I hear, but it's her body he's guarding. She likes the tennis pro at the club. After a while I decided I didn't care for it, so I broke off from her."

"A lot of men prefer younger women."

"That's different."

"A lot of women prefer younger men. I'm told it's quite fashionable, in fact."

"I'm not one of those women."

"Did she have an eye for Billy?"

She gave me a cold look, then let it fade and shrugged. "You're astute. Yes, I thought she was more interested in him than she needed to be, and I didn't like it. I wanted him away from his old companions, so I took him and left."

"And sent him off for a cure of his own."

"Not right away. At first we deceived ourselves by thinking that he'd give up the drugs on his own. But of course he hadn't. He pretended to, but he hadn't. After that we sent him to a private hospital."

"And he came back cured."

"Yes. He was accepted at Brown and he's doing quite well."

"And nobody he once knew might want him dead?"

"No."

I got up and so did she. At the door she said, "I really think that Susie is quite wrong. All I can imagine is that she's in some kind of shock. She was very fond of Jim Norris, and she and Billy are close. The accident must have disturbed her very much indeed."

We exchanged good-byes and I left. As I drove I wished I hadn't stopped smoking. There was a drug bust coming up and there was the explosion, and there was Susie

Martin saying there was a link between the explosion and drugs but the chief and Marge Martin saying there was no such link. Maybe the chief was lying just to keep me from nosing around and screwing up the impending bust, but then again maybe he wasn't. If Billy was a squealer, why didn't the chief just tell me? If he'd done that, I'd probably have agreed to keep my nose out of things until the bust was history, and then maybe he and I together could have looked into the theory that Billy had been set up for murder. But the chief didn't act like a man with a murder to solve. He was directing traffic and riding around in the cruiser and acting as normal as a policeman can who knows that the big state and federal guns are about to swoop down on his community. Ah, how I missed my old corncob pipe!

I went home and called Quinn in Boston, but he was out. So much for that angle. So much for every angle. I had just enough time to make Wasque Point. I got into the Landcruiser and headed for the fishing ground. I thought back five years and reminded myself that I'd left police work behind me quite consciously, quite deliberately, because I was tired of trouble and no longer believed that I could or should devote myself to curing society of its ills. Rather, I'd live within myself and seek the simple life, close to earth and sea, apart from human foible and folly. It seemed as good a plan now as it had then. I was glad when I got to the beach.

Zee's Jeep was gone from Wasque, but there were a dozen others with fish tossed in their shade. Three- or four-pounders. I watched for a while. There was more coffee drinking going on than fishing, so things must have slowed down. I got out and took my graphite and put on a three-ounce red-headed Roberts. I'd added about fifteen yards to my cast when I'd gotten the graphite. It was a sweet rod. I walked down to the water, put a little muscle into the cast, and dropped the Roberts far out into the edge of the rip.

Bingo!

In about ten seconds I was shoulder to shoulder with other fishermen. It's a well-known fact that there are fishermen living under the sand at Wasque. You can be down there all alone, and as soon as you catch a fish they all jump out and start casting right beside you. When the fish are gone, the people all disappear again.

Zee should be here, I found myself thinking. I got eleven fish on twice that many casts and then they were gone. Ten minutes later I got a final stray and called it a day. We all talked for a while.

"Hey, J.W., I hear you hauled George Martin off the beach yesterday. He okay?"

I said he was as good as could be expected. George was popular on the beach. He had more money than all of the rest of us together could ever hope to have, but he was just another fisherman as far as the regulars were concerned.

"Too damned bad about Jim Norris."

"Yeah."

"I hear he was leaving the island and going home. Never make it now except in a box."

"George and Jim were good buddies. Fished together a lot when Jim wasn't working."

"George going to make it, J.W.?"

"He says he'll be on the beach as soon as they let him out of bed."

"That's George. He'd rather fish than fuck."

"He'd rather fish *and* fuck."

"Yeah, that's probably more like it."

Everybody laughed. It came to me that Zee had said she'd gotten off work at two in the morning, which probably meant that she went to work at six in the evening.

"It's fish in the freezer time," I said. I tossed my catch into the box, drove to Herring Creek and scaled them, then went home. I filleted them on the bench behind my storage shed, bagged them, and put all but one in the freezer. The one I put in the fridge. I like fresh bluefish a lot about three times each spring. After that I still eat it because that's what I have, but not because I particularly like it. But I never get tired of smoked bluefish, so I freeze it for that purpose. Down my driveway I'm famous for my smoked bluefish.

I went back and washed off the fish-cleaning bench and tossed the bluefish carcasses into the woods northeast of the house. In a week the bones would be bare; meanwhile, the prevailing southwesterlies would keep the stench away.

I mixed up some stuffing and layered it between the two fillets I'd put in the fridge and put the fish on an oiled cookie sheet. Stuffed bluefish! Yum. Too much for one meal for one man, but delicious again tomorrow, warmed over. I popped a Molson and took it out to the garden with me while I picked peas. Pods, actually. The sweet Chinese kind. Back inside I put them in a pan with salted water. While everything cooked, I finished the beer and got a sauterne out of the fridge. I like it better than drier stuff with bluefish. I took a swig. Good! I poured a glass for the cook. When the timer dinged, I put everything on the table and turned on the radio to listen to the news.

I have a tendency to eat fast when I'm alone, so I took my time, just as though I had company. I imagined Zee sitting across the table. It was a nice bit of imagining. The radio news seemed about the same as usual. Once I'd experimented and hadn't listened to it for a month. When I listened again, nothing much had changed. Still, I kept on listening to it. A human voice at mealtime.

When I was through, I washed and stacked the dishes and called Quinn. He was still out. Probably in a bar somewhere doing newspaper work. Quinn was okay. I was okay, too. The wine bottle was empty and in the trash basket under the kitchen counter. I got into the Landcruiser and drove to Oak Bluffs. It was dusk and the beach was empty save for stragglers who hated to go home for supper. A lone surf-sailer was easing along in the dying wind and beyond him, out in the sound, sails were white against the darkening sky, trying for harbor before nightfall.

In the hospital parking lot I found Zee's Jeep. George's Wagoneer, too. Susie must still be visiting. Personally, I hate hospitals. They're unhealthy places. People die there all the time. I almost did myself. I went into the emergency ward and immediately saw Zee. She was saying good-night to a patient with a patch over his eye. Another Vineyard casualty of some sort. I decided to try the direct approach.

"Hello," I said.

6

"Well, hello, Jeff." She looked terrific in a newly pressed white uniform. The doctors in emergency often look like they just came in from the farm or the beach. An informal crew. Zee looked professional.

"Can I talk to you even though there's nothing wrong with me?"

"Who told you there was nothing wrong with you?" She had fine teeth. Very even and white.

"I went fishing this afternoon. I noticed that you got your Jeep back from the beach."

"You're not the only man that I know." I could believe that. "A couple of friends went down and brought it to me."

"It's good for a woman to know a number of manly four-wheel-drive driving men."

"Like you."

"Pardon my shy smile and my foot scuffing the floor."

"You still have my rod and tacklebox."

"And your waders, too."

"Ah, yes. The ten-pound bag."

"Everything's out in my manly FWD. I'll stick your gear in your Jeep when I leave. Say, how long are you going to be on this shift?"

"Two o'clock in the morning, just like yesterday. Why do you ask? she inquired coyly."

"I thought I might invite you out to dinner so you could get to know me better and maybe I could get you drunk so you'd do something your mother would regret. Or, barring that, maybe I might just invite you out to dinner. But since you get off at two in the morning, maybe I should invite you to breakfast instead, or maybe to a snack or something. . . ."

"Well?"

"Well, what?"

"Well, do it. Invite me. But not to breakfast or a snack. I'm really wiped out and I expect to be more wiped out when I get through this shift. Try supper."

"You mean I spent my teenage years wondering how to ask girls out and all I had to do was just come right out and ask?"

"What can you lose?"

"You might say no, and I'd be crushed. Beneath this brawny chest beats a sensitive heart."

"How Hemingwayesque. Take a chance."

"Okay. Will you go out to dinner with me?"

"Yes."

"Golly." I felt terrific. "When?"

"I'm off tomorrow night. The next morning I go on day shift again."

"Where do you like to eat?"

"You decide. Be manly."

"I can't help it most of the time, but the sight of you turns me into a child."

"In that case I'll reconsider my answer."

"I was lying. I'm more masculine than you can possibly imagine. You'll trust my choice of restaurants?"

"If you can't trust the man who teaches you how to cast, whom can you trust?"

She lived in West Tisbury. An up-islander. I got directions and also her telephone number. A double score. I told her I'd pick her up at six-thirty. About then a woman with torn clothes and a bloody knee was brought in.

"Moped accident number five for the day," said Zee, and she was gone.

I walked back through the corridors of the hospital and found Billy's room. No armed guards. No guards of any kind. The chief obviously hadn't taken my suggestion about possible murder in the hospital very seriously. Neither had I, for that matter. Still, if I walked in with, say, a silenced .22, I could walk right out again without a soul to stop me. I went to the door and heard voices from inside. Billy's and a female's. I thought it was Susie's, but then I knew it wasn't. It was a jittery voice, a tight voice. I couldn't make out the words, but I recognized the tones. I'd heard voices like that in Boston long ago. I knocked on the door and walked in.

The girl jerked around. She'd been sitting on the bed, and now she jumped off. Her eyes were flickering, like those of a scared cat. Her hands leaped into a knot. Billy stared at me.

"Oops," I said. "Gee, Billy, I didn't know you had company."

"Well, I do," he said after a moment.

"My name's Jackson," I said, giving the girl a fast smile. "I'm a friend of the family."

She nodded and put on a quick smile of her own.

"This . . . this is Julie," said Billy. "She's my . . . a friend from college. She . . ."

"I heard about the accident," she said in a startled-fawn way. "It was on the news. I came over to see him. I was so worried." One hand rubbed the opposite arm, then found the other hand and knotted into it again. She looked quickly at Billy. "Well, maybe I should go. I guess I really should. I guess I will. I'll . . . I'll see you later, then, Billy. Okay?"

Julie went out. I smiled at Billy. "Just came by to see how you're doing, kid."

"Fine," he said, "I'm doing fine."

"That's the way, kid. I'll see you later, then."

"Yeah. Yeah, thanks for coming by."

I went out and down the hall and out into the parking lot. A Mazda two-door was pulling out. Julie was in it. A teacher I knew in Boston told me that you could always tell the difference between the faculty cars and the student cars. The student cars were new.

Julie was down the road a piece when I drove out of the parking lot in the Landcruiser. She didn't spot me in the rearview mirror and lead me on a high-speed chase like on TV. Instead, she drove down Circuit Avenue, parked, and went into the Fireside Bar. By the time I found a parking place, she'd been in there awhile.

When I went in, I bumped right into Bonzo. Bonzo wasn't his name, but that's what people called him because he liked Ronald Reagan's last movie so much. Also because he'd blown away a good part of his brain on bad acid and hadn't been too swift since. Not as smart as the Bonzo in the movie, in fact. I'd never known him before he'd popped acid, but I'd heard that he'd been a smart kid. Once I'd taken him fishing and it had been like taking a child. He'd been my buddy ever since. Bonzo earned his keep by scrubbing floors and doing odd jobs at the Fireside.

"Hi, J.W.," he said. "Long time no see." He grinned, showing pretty good teeth for a guy in his condition. His mother probably made him brush every day. Bonzo shook my hand. "Hi, J.W.," he said again. "Say, when are we going fishing again?"

Just then Julie came out of the ladies' room. In this case it was identified by a stencil of a little girl pulling up her panties. The men's room was adorned with a stencil of a little boy trying to button up his pants. Or unbutton them. It was hard to tell. Julie looked different. Gone was her nervousness. She looked laid back and at ease. She went to the bar and I heard her joke with the bartender. Her voice was low and smooth.

"Later," I said to Bonzo. "We'll go fishing later."

I went to the bar and sat beside Julie.

She looked like the all-American girl. Sandy blond hair, unlined face, clean blouse, plaid skirt, and sandals. She gave me a smile of nonrecognition. Her brain was in second gear and shifting down.

"Hi, Julie," I said. "Billy told me I could find you here."

"Billy told you?" The light dawned. "Oh, yeah. You're the guy I met in the hospital. Hi, there." She grinned. She was feeling better all the time. The bartender set a pink drink in front of her. She sipped it through a straw. The bartender looked at me. I ordered a beer.

"I've got to talk to you," I said. "There's a booth over there. Come on, it's important."

"Booth? Important? Oh, okay—why not?" Mellow and getting mellower, she smiled. I escorted her and her drink to the booth, went back for my beer, and then sat down across from her. Around us the noises and smells of the early-evening crowd made a wall. I leaned across to her.

"Billy sent me after you. I need something!" I made my hands tremble and I darted my eyes around. "I just need a little. Just to get me through, you know? He said I could get it from you. That you had it."

She stared at me with a dreamy look. I let my fingers dance to her arm, then dance away again. I licked my lips and chewed a bit on my lower one.

"He didn't have anything, of course. He couldn't have, because they'd have found it in his clothes, but he'd have given me some if he'd had it, you understand? He said to see you! Look, Julie, I have money. I'll pay you. But I need it now, you know? Please!"

She tried to be intelligent. "Who are you?" She wrinkled her forehead at me and sipped her pink drink.

"You know me. I'm J. W. Jackson. We met in Billy's room. I was just looking for something to calm me down, you know? I mean my main man is off island, that's the trouble. But I knew Billy and he told me I could talk to you."

"Did he?"

"Call him up, for God's sake! He'll tell you! Here! Here's some change . . ." I fumbled in my pocket. "Just call him, please!" I had a pretty good whine, I thought. Maybe I could make it onstage or the silver screen or on the street with a tin cup.

"Hey, hey," Julie said, putting her hand on my arm. "It's okay, man. Hey, I believe you. I've been there myself, you know?" Her voice was gentle, concerned. She cared for me or maybe what she saw as my condition. "Not here," she said. "Too many people. Most of them look okay, but you never know, you know?"

I wondered how many times the two of us would say "you know" if we were not interrupted for, say, the next hour. A hundred? A thousand? "I've got a car," I said. "We could use it."

"Okay," she said with a gentle smile. "Drink your beer."

"I don't want any beer," I said. "I want . . ."

"All right." She smiled. "Take it easy, man. We'll go."

We went. She walked as if she were on air, giving me compassionate looks. I wondered what she was on, and ran the cornucopia of popular drugs through my mind. I was five years out of date, but I imagined things hadn't changed that much. Whatever she used, I was going to get some.

"When you feel better, maybe we can come back," she said, taking my arm. "Billy says the Fireside is a good place. Felt good to me, that's for sure." She laughed. I hurried us along.

"What's this sort of car?" she asked when we got there.

"Never mind. Just get in. Oh, hell, it's a Landcruiser, a sort of Japanese Jeep." We got in. We were parked under a tree in the shadow cast by the streetlights. Nobody was around. I fumbled out my wallet and spilled some bills into my lap. "Here," I said. "Hurry!"

"Hey, take it easy, man. Roll up your sleeve. You want me to do it or do you want to do it yourself?"

"I don't care! I'll do it myself. What do you have?"

She opened her purse and took out a plastic syringe and a needle packaged in a sealed envelope. "Codeine. Look. My old man's a doctor. I get these from his office. Sterile. Neat, huh? You can't be too careful, you know? I only use them once, then I get rid of them." She got out a vial of liquid. "You'll be okay in just a few minutes, J.W. Just relax."

"I'll do it," I said, taking the syringe and the vial. I took them, looked at them, and put them in my pocket. Julie didn't understand. Then she did understand. She put a hand to her mouth and bit lightly on her finger.

"Oh, God," she said. "Oh, God!"

* 7 *

I tried to look like stone. "Ever been in jail, Julie?"

"Oh, God," she said. "No. Oh, God . . ."

"Your parents know about this, Julie?"

"No. Oh, God . . ."

Time for the carrot. "They don't need to know, Julie. But I do. You're a nice kid, I think, but I'm not nice. You understand me? Talk to me?"

"A narc," she said, beginning to cry. "A narc. Oh, God . . ."

I reached across and took her purse. She held on to it for a moment, then let it go. Inside were half a dozen more syringes and another vial. I found her wallet and took out her driver's license. Julie Potter. I put the license in my pocket and flipped through the wallet. A student I.D. card from Brown, pictures of a family of five. Healthy Americans. Julie was the eldest child. Mom and Dad were clean-cut post-preppy types. Behind them was the house. Colonial. A country place. I found her father's card. William Potter, M.D. It had addresses and telephone numbers. I put it in my pocket with the license. Then I took out the other syringes and the vial and added them to my collection. My pockets were beginning to bulge. Beside me, Julie's head was down and her shoulders were shaking.

"I don't think you're in too deep yet, Julie. You still have good skin tone, your hair still has a shine to it, and you've still got meat on your bones. You hear me?"

She nodded, sobbing. I found a little package of tissues in her purse and gave them to her, then put the purse back in her lap. She cried into a tissue.

"You didn't get this stuff on the island, did you?"

She shook her head.

"Where'd you get it, Julie?"

"I won't tell you!" She had a bit of spunk I'd have to get rid of.

"Julie, you just tried to sell me this stuff. Your parents will have to know about it if we charge you."

She caught the "if" the way a bluefish takes a hook.

"What do you mean 'if'?"

"I mean that if you talk to me I may not have to bring you into things at all. I mean you're just an amateur, a small-time user. I'll take you in if I can't do any better, but I'm really interested in some other people. Maybe you can help me."

If I hadn't given up smoking, I could light up right now and blow a few tough smoke rings while Julie suffered. Instead, I just sat there, hoping that she was thinking about scandal at school and at home.

"I . . . I get it at school. How can I trust you? Oh, God . . ."

"You can trust me. Talk to me and I forget I ever met you. You have my word."

"Your word!"

"My word."

She cried for a little longer.

"Okay," I said. "We'll go down to the station, then. . . ."

"No! No. I . . . I don't know very much, I swear. Some of

us use a little now and then, you know? We get it at school. Brown's tough sometimes, and we have to unwind. Weekends. Parties. I smoked a little in prep school. I mean, is there anybody under forty who hasn't at least tried grass? But I'm not really a user. I mean, I've tried this and that, but I don't . . ." She wiped at her face with more tissues.

"Who's your supplier?"

"Nobody. Everybody. It's around."

"Grass may be around, coke may be around, pills may be around. But this stuff isn't around."

"Billy," she said. "Billy has it."

Billy.

"He brought it around. We liked it. I love him, you know."

According to her driver's license she was nineteen. As I remembered, it was a hard time to be alive. A lot of passion, mixed-up thoughts, problems. "That's why you came over to see him. You love him. You love your dealer."

She flamed up. "He's not my dealer! He's just a boy who—" She stopped, furious.

"You said in his room that you'd heard about the accident, but that was a lie, wasn't it?"

"What do you mean?" Her anger was suddenly on hold.

"I mean it's pretty unlikely that you'd just heard about an accident on Martha's Vineyard when you live down in Connecticut. The Connecticut news doesn't include stories like that. No, Billy telephoned you and asked you to come up."

"All right, all right. What difference does it make?"

"It makes a little difference. You brought him some of your needles and dope, didn't you?"

"No!"

"It'll be easy to check. If he's got the fixings, they'll be right there in his room. The way I see it is this: He's hurting and he's in a hospital room where he can't get anything from his normal supplier, so he calls you to bring him some of the stuff you got from him in the first place. You bring it to him, too, because you love him and you don't like to have him hurt. That's about the way it happened, I imagine."

"Please . . ."

I waited while she cried some more. Then: "Where does he get his stuff? I mean when he isn't getting it from you."

"I don't know, I don't know."

"Billy likes to have people know he's somebody important. He reminds people like the guys who work in the boatyard that his old man has money. That's the way he is. I'll bet that he's dropped a hint or two about his source. Let me help you. His source is on the island, isn't it?"

"I don't know what you're talking about."

"Sure you do. Billy lives on the island. His contacts are here. He hasn't been on the mainland long enough to tie into the Providence drug circles, so I know he gets his stuff here. But I need to know a name. Give me a name and you walk."

"Sylvia, he mentioned Sylvia. I don't know what her last name is."

"Why do you think it's a woman?"

Julie looked at me with genuine surprise. "What do you mean? Who else but a woman would be named Sylvia?"

It was clear that Julie and her family did not mingle with the Connecticut Portuguese.

"Never mind," I said. I got out her license and her

father's business card and gave them back to her. Then I dug out the syringes and the vials. "Do you want these?"

"Nobody wants them right after a fix," she said bitterly. "Everybody's strong then." She stared at her hands. "You keep them."

"Get some help. Somebody at Brown can point you to the right people."

"Sure."

"Or you might try trusting your father to help you. Whatever you decide, I'd change my circle of friends if I were you. You're young and pretty and probably fairly smart, but you won't be any of those things if you hang around Billy and his pals."

"Yeah." She got out and walked down Circuit Avenue. I wrote down the information from her license and her father's card before I forgot it. Then I put the vial and syringes in the glove compartment and drove home.

There I put the drug stuff in a paper bag in the fridge, put on a Willie Nelson tape, and poured myself a Rémy Martin. One of my luxuries. No jug brandies for J. W. Jackson. I wear old clothes and my car is fourteen years old, but I drink Rémy Martin, by God! Sometimes, anyway.

Willie sang about Poncho and Lefty and about fishing and growing old and I thought about my day. I realized that I'd liked it. I'd liked nosing around. It felt good. Natural. It had been six years since I'd done it professionally and I'd never planned to do it again, but today I had and it felt pretty good. I ran everything through my mind, turned the tape over, and thought some more while Willie sang. When Willie was through, I went to bed.

I woke early, thinking of Zee. I got up and made four loaves of Betty Crocker white bread and set it to rise. I took scallops out of the freezer to thaw. I was at the A&P when it opened and bought leeks, onions, ice cream, canned peach halves, frozen raspberries, cream, butter (unsalted, of course), and fresh asparagus. When Al's Package Store opened across the street, I bought a bottle of cherry liqueur and a good Graves.

Home again, I set the raspberries to thaw, then made a cream of refrigerator soup with the leeks, some butter and milk, a potato, and whatever leftover vegetables I could find in the fridge. Green vichyssoise, sort of, with salt and pepper and thyme for seasoning. Then I made a scallops St.-Jacques and flavored it with parsley, sage, no rosemary, and thyme. And basil.

I had a beer and punched down the bread, and after it had risen again put it in the oven. By noon it was finished, and I had eaten nearly half a loaf. There is nothing, simply nothing, better than fresh hot bread and butter. When the bread was cool, I put two loaves in the freezer and then had most of the other half of the open loaf with more beer and some ham and cheese.

Supper was ready. The wine was in the fridge. I'd make the peach melba at the last minute. It was only one o'clock. What efficiency.

I got out my *Gazette* again. The captain of the *Bluefin* was named Tim Mello. He lived in Vineyard Haven. I called his number. Nobody home. I decided to find the boat.

Vineyard Haven is where most of the ferries from the mainland come in, much to the annoyance of many business people in Oak Bluffs who wish even more ferries landed there so they could make even more money from

day trippers. Vineyard Haven is not particularly island-
ish or nautical or even quaint. It looks a lot like any other
little New England town, but it's located on the Vineyard
so it's not really like a mainland town. Out on West Chop
there are a lot of big houses, for instance, and the harbor
has more schooners in it than any harbor I know of.
Vineyard Haven is also the traffic jam capital of Martha's
Vineyard.

I got through the traffic jam and eventually found the
Bluefin lying at a dock not far from the shipyard. I parked
beside a little red M.G. sportscar. Beyond the *Bluefin* rose
the masts of the yachts lying inside the breakwater. The
biggest masts belonged to the *Shenandoah*, the lovely old
hermaphrodite brig that cruises the south coast of New
England in the summer. Someday I plan to play tourist
and take a sail on her myself. But not today.

The *Bluefin* was sixty-five feet long and equipped with a
pulpit, outriggers, and more electronic gear than I imagined existed. She was a beauty, the sort of boat rarely
owned by individuals anymore, but by corporations. She
had a black hull and teak everything else. Tim Mello, her
captain, was a young fellow, which means younger than
me. Most cops are, too. So are a lot of other people, a fact
that perplexes me. How did it happen? I remember when
almost everybody was older than me.

I asked Mello for permission to board and he waved a
hand. He was installing a new loran. Something better
than the billion-dollar one that they'd gotten by on before,
I supposed.

Mello laughed. "I didn't buy it, I just run the boat. What
can you do for me?"

A jester of my own caliber. "Ask not what your country
can do for you, but what you can do for et cetera," I said.

"Okay, what can I do for my country, in this case you?"

I told him that I represented a member of the Martin family and that I wanted to talk about the rescue of Billy Martin.

"I made a full statement to the police. I imagine you can get it. If you're an insurance agent, you'll be better off talking with the corporation lawyer."

"I'm not anything official or unofficial. Billy Martin's sister asked me to find out anything I can about the accident. I've seen the cops, I've seen the guys at the boatyard in Edgartown, and I've seen the Martins, and now I'm seeing you."

"Okay," he said, "fire away. You don't mind if I keep on working, I hope."

I didn't mind.

"I had a party of two," he said. "They wanted to go bluefishing in the Wasque rip. They came down about eight and we left. I could see a boat coming out of Edgartown as we got closer to Cape Pogue. I knew he'd have to go outside the shallows off the point, so I hooked out a little. I wasn't really watching the boat, but the people in my party were. They say she just blew up. I saw the flash from the corner of my eye and turned just as the boom got to us. I saw somebody in the water, thrashing around. I went in as close as I dared and got hold of him with a boathook and pulled him aboard. He was pretty singed, and he was yelling about his friend Jim. I circled as close as I could, but I didn't see anybody else in the water, so I radioed a mayday to the Coast Guard and to the Edgartown harbormaster. Then I got worried about the survivor. Burns and shock. He didn't look too good. So I radioed for an ambulance to meet us in Oak Bluffs. This baby can do mega-knots, and she did them all on that trip." He looked up from his work. "That's about it. Say, can you get a hand under there and fit this nut on that bolt?"

I could and did. "Who else was with you? Who was in the fishing party? I'd like to talk to them, too."

"Here. Use this wrench to hold the nut while I tighten it from here with the screwdriver. Their name is Sarusa. Nice old couple. Over from New Bedford. Never been boat fishing before. Never got to go this time either, because they had to go back home that same afternoon. They were pretty excited. Rescue at sea and all that. They're probably telling their grandchildren about it whenever they get the chance."

We tightened another bolt together. "Who owns this floating palace?" I asked. "I may send them a bill."

"I'll pay you with a beer. Fred Sylvia gives me my orders, but Brunner International actually owns it. Business expense. The executives use it to entertain clients. Sometimes the wives and kids get a ride, too. Occasionally we charter. This was one of those times."

"Did you take the charter?"

"Me? Never! Fred Sylvia calls me and the party shows up and I take them wherever I'm told. In this case I got the call on Saturday for a Monday morning trip. Two days' advance warning, at least. Sometimes I get less."

"Where's headquarters?"

"My checks come from New York, but they've got offices all over the world." He grinned and we admired our work. "How about that beer? The sun is over the yardarm."

We went below, and he got two Watneys out of a refrigerator bigger than mine in a galley bigger than my kitchen. We sat in chairs designed by someone who actually knew how human bodies are built and what it took to relax them.

"Not bad, eh?" Mello smiled. "Robbie Burns may have had a high opinion of honest poverty, but as for me, I'd rather be rich."

"Where does the help live?"

"Up forward. Spartan quarters. Merely elegant, not luxurious. I suffer up there as best I can when the bosses are on board, but when the cat's away the mouse plays out here."

"Maybe someday you'll meet a corporate daughter who'll fall madly in love with you. You'll get married and become the principal heir to the principal stockholder and all of this will be yours."

"Yeah," he said, "good plan."

"When it happens, will you hire me for your old job?"

"Sure," he said, "I wouldn't consider anyone else."

We drank our Watneys. "I don't recall ever seeing the *Bluefin* on the Wasque rips," I said.

"She's never been on the Wasque rips. *Bluefin* is made for tuna, sword, marlin, that sort of thing. But my orders were to go to Wasque, so that's where we were going. They call me a captain, but I'm only a slave. You're not the only one to think Wasque's an odd place to fish in the *Bluefin*. The guys at the Fireside had a good laugh when I told them about it Saturday night."

I couldn't think of anything else to ask him, so I finished my beer, thanked him, and left.

I stopped at the hospital on my way home and saw George. He looked good. "Fish are still in," I said.

"Save some for me."

"You're kidding. I'm getting all I can while I have the

chance. I've been trying to outfish you for five years, and if they keep you in here long enough I may get enough of a head start that you'll never catch up. This is my year."

Susie walked in. She kissed her father, then turned to me. "Hi, J.W. How's it going?"

Code talk. "It's going okay. If I achieve any major breakthroughs in my life, you'll be the first to know." It was a lie, but not one I had to think about very much. Besides, maybe it wasn't really a lie because I hadn't really achieved any breakthroughs. I mean, no real Breakthroughs with a capital B.

I tried to look honest and trustworthy, and she managed a smile. "Please do." She turned to her father.

Down the hall I stuck my head into Billy's room. He seemed asleep. No Julie. Maybe she'd taken my advice to seek a better class of companion. Maybe not. I went home and called Boston.

"Well?" I asked Quinn.

"Well, what?"

"Well, what's the guy's name?"

"Don't know. People are being very cagey. About all I've got is that whatever's happening looks like it's happening next week. Jesus, J.W., I got other work to do, you know. There are seven million stories in the naked city, and I'm not on that one."

"Okay, okay. Tell me about Brunner International."

"What?"

"Brunner International. What is it? Who runs it? Where is it? Stuff like that. Everything you can tell me."

"Why don't you buy a *Wall Street Journal*, you cheap bastard?"

"I'm spending all my money on my telephone bill."

I rang off and got out my *Gazette* again. It was beginning to look pretty worn. I cut out the stories about the accident so I could carry them around with me. There was no telling what I might need to know next. By this time, I knew, Sam Spade would have solved my problem, but Sam was not around. He never is when you need him.

* 8 *

According to the *Gazette*, the passengers on the *Bluefin* were Manuel and Alice Sarusa of New Bedford. When I phoned her, Mrs. Sarusa was delighted to tell me of her adventure. I finally managed to ask her how they happened to charter the *Bluefin* and why they decided to go to Wasque when they could have gone a lot farther for their money.

"Well," said Mrs. Sarusa, "Manny used to fish off the beach at Wasque when he was a young fellow, and he always envied those men out there in the boats, so when Freddy Sylvia—that's Manny's cousin who lives there in Vineyard Haven, you probably heard of him, he works for Brunner, the big outfit, you know?—so anyway, when Freddy charters the company boat for us on our fiftieth, naturally Manny wanted to finally go fishing off Wasque!"

"Brunner International?"

"That's the one. Freddy's a very big man there, but with us, well, he's just folks. You know what I mean? Just family. He set the whole thing up for us. Got us the boat, bought us tickets to the island, arranged everything. A real gentleman of the old school, like I told Manny . . ."

By the time I was able to hang up, the phone company owned my soul. I looked up Fred Sylvia's number. It wasn't there. There were a couple of dozen Sylvias, but no Fred in Vineyard Haven. I wasn't discouraged; even some natives have unlisted numbers.

I had a beer and put a bottle of vodka in the freezer. Icy martinis on order if demanded by my guest-to-be. I considered Fred Sylvia, cousin of Manny Sarusa. A gentleman of the old school, husband of Maria who liked young men, father of Danny who'd gotten Billy Martin hooked on drugs before taking the cure himself. I wondered if Tim Mello, youthful captain of the *Bluefin*, was Maria's type. If so, maybe he didn't need to wait for a corporation daughter to fall for him.

I went out to the garden, yanked out a few weeds, pulled up a radish to see if they were big enough for salads (they weren't), and turned on the water. Beyond the garden I had a good view of Nantucket Sound. It was filled with sail. I wanted a sailboat and was trying to save for one, but couldn't afford it yet. Or maybe I could, but just hadn't gotten around to buying it yet. I hadn't gotten around to doing very much of anything for the past five years. I imagined Zee and me in a sailboat out there. We didn't look bad. The sky was blue, the wind was fifteen knots on the beam, the air warm, the sun shining. The way sailing ought to be. If you're going to imagine something, imagine something good. I hardly knew her, but Zee seemed to be invading my fantasies.

Back inside, I put the asparagus in a dish. If you want good asparagus, the best way to cook it is in a 300-degree oven: you rinse it, trim it, salt and pepper it and dot it with butter, cover it with foil, and bake it for half an hour. When I got it covered, I put it in the fridge, got another beer, and phoned Quinn.

"Gee, Quinn, what are you doing in the office this time

of day? I figured you'd be out belting down a few in the grand tradition of hard-drinking, tough but honest journalists."

"Screw you," said Quinn. "You know, I'll be glad when whatever you're doing down there is done. I can't stand many more of these calls. I'm being communicated to death."

"Does the name Fred Sylvia ring any bells?"

"No. Why?"

"Drop it around and see if it bounces. He may be your Vineyard main man. Or maybe he isn't. If he's on the list, I'd like to know."

"Golly, is this a clue?"

"Just an anonymous tip to a crusading newspaperman. Let me know, okay?"

"Anything else?"

"Brunner International?"

"Nothing yet."

"Fred Sylvia works for them."

"Ah."

I hung up. It was time. I drove up island to West Tisbury to find Zee. West Tisbury used to be part of Tisbury, but isn't anymore. Now it's its own town. It consists of a general store, the county fair grounds, a church, and houses containing people who don't go down to Edgartown or Oak Bluffs much except to buy booze. West Tisbury people tend to stay there. They like it. So do I. On Saturdays there's a farmers' market at the fair grounds where you can get great fresh vegetables, flowers, and baked goods. The best smoked bluefish around used to be available there before an overzealous health inspector decided to sic federal commercial regulations on the cottage-industry types. Across the street is an art gallery beside a little field full of dancing statues. Whenever I learn that somebody is on the Vineyard for the first time, I tell them to go up and have a look at the statues. They make you feel good.

Zee lived in a little house down a long, sandy road. She rented it from somebody.

"Hi," she said. She wore a blue dress and white shoes with low heels. Her hair, which had been pulled back the other two times I'd seen her, fell down around her shoulders. It was shiny and dark and thick.

"Wow," I said. She smiled. I opened the Landcruiser's door and she got in.

"Where are we going?" she asked.

"A private club. Members only."

We drove to Edgartown and went down my road. She didn't look nervous. I pulled into my yard and stopped.

"Terrific," said Zee, and she jumped out. "Your place?"

"My place. Excellent cheap food."

"Do I get a guided tour before we eat?"

"You get a tour as soon as I get a beer. You make my throat dry."

"I'll come with you and see the inside first. You can get me a beer, too. Why did you say that?"

"What?"

"That your throat was dry."

"I don't know. I guess I just didn't want you not to know."

We went inside. My fishing rods were hung across the ceiling. It suddenly seemed to me to be a pretty rough place—worn chairs, beat-up books, locked gun case, a couch that sagged.

"Can I wander?"

"Sure." I got two beers and set everything in the fridge

out to warm a bit before I cooked it. I found her in the spare bedroom looking at my father's best decoy. "My dad made that," I said. "He bought this place a long time ago when prices were really low. He was a hunter and a fisherman and he liked to carve. When he died, I inherited the place. Good thing for me; I couldn't afford it now."

We went outside and I showed her the garden and the workshop in the shed out back and the smoker and fillet bench behind that and my grape vines and fruit trees. Then we went up onto the balcony above the porch and looked out at the Sound. Late boats were leaning into the dying wind, heading for Edgartown. We sat down in chairs and looked at the ocean.

"It's beautiful."

"A million-dollar view." I went down and got more beer and came up again. We talked for a while, and then she said, "You know, my throat was dry, too. I just wanted you to know."

When the sun went down behind the oaks, it began to get chilly, so we went down into the house.

"You sit," I said. "I cook. The kitchen isn't big enough for two even if I'd let you try to help."

I put the St.-Jacques and the asparagus in the oven, set the table, and sliced the bread. When everything was ready I opened the wine and called her in. I gave her small portions of everything and was glad when she had seconds. Afterward I made coffee and peach melba for dessert. Then we had Rémy Martin in front of the fireplace. I was nervous and comfortable at the same time. It was as though I hadn't brought a woman to the house before. We talked.

About ten-thirty I took her home.

"It's early," she said. Was there a slight look of hurt in her eyes?

"I know. But you have to work tomorrow and I want this evening to end too soon so I can ask you out again."

"All right, Jefferson." She smiled.

"It's my date," I said. "I get to run it the way I want to."

In West Tisbury she asked me if I wanted a nightcap. "No," I said. "I want to be able to wonder about what your place looks like."

Then I was leaning forward and she wasn't leaning back and our lips touched. Mine were dry. I felt about fifteen years old. It was terrific.

"Good night," I said. "Thank you."

She was standing in front of her door watching as I drove away. She was smiling. I fought an impulse to turn around and accept her invitation. Instead, I rolled down my window and shouted, "Don't forget to practice your casts!"

Some long-forgotten sensations had obviously turned my brain to mush. Feeling red-faced and oafish, I drove back to Edgartown. I could only hope that she liked idiots.

* 9 *

Fred Sylvia lived on West Chop, according to the records in the Vineyard Haven town hall. I drove down the side street that led to his place. A large, comfortable house of weathered shingles, white trim, and brick fireplaces, it was set on an acre or two of lawns, shrubs, and trees and overlooked Vineyard Haven harbor. In front of the house was a shiny new tan Buick two-door. Sylvia believed in buying American. Across the harbor, as crowded with power yachts and sailboats as other harbors on the east coast, I could see the dock where the *Bluefin* was lying. At the foot of Sylvia's land there was a beach and a small dock. Tied to the dock were a motorboat and a small sailboat. It was a very nice view.

That morning Quinn had had news. "Sylvia isn't the only name," he'd said, "but it's one of the big ones. I asked a guy and he asked me where I'd gotten the name. I didn't tell him, but I did tell everything to my editor and now I'm on the story. So I may see you in a few days. Any fish left?"

"For you, an ocean full," I said. "What about Brunner International?"

"A big outfit. Importing, exporting, commodities, movies, you name it. Offices here, in Europe, South America,

and the Middle East. H.Q. is in New York. Sylvia is about
halfway up the ladder. One of those sharp guys you never
see up front. I'm not sure what he does, but he does
something profitable."

Profitable indeed. I admired his house, his car, his boats,
and his lawn. According to census figures, Sylvia and his
wife had two grown children besides Danny. Maybe Danny
would manage to grow up, too, sometime. I walked up to
the front door and rang the bell. I heard it chime
somewhere inside.

A tall, black-haired woman opened the door. She was
wearing tennis whites. She looked like a model.

"Yes?" Her eyes went down and came up again. I hadn't
dressed for the occasion, but I gave her my best smile.

"I'd like to speak to Mr. Fred Sylvia, please."

She eyed my clothes again. "Well, you're certainly not a
salesman."

"No, ma'am. It's a private matter. Business."

Was I too old for her? Maybe she was just anxious to get
to the court. It was a nice day for tennis. Anyway, she
stepped back and I stepped in. She picked up her racket
and called down the hall, "Leon, there's a man here to see
Fred. I'm going down to the club. Sit down, Mr. . . ."

"Jackson."

"Sit down, Mr. Jackson. Leon will take you to my
husband."

"Thank you, Mrs. Sylvia. Have a good game."

"I'll do my best, Mr. Jackson." She went down to the
Buick and got behind the wheel. Great body! I heard a
floorboard squeak and turned to face a very large young
man with a thick neck. I shut the front door. The large
man wore an alligator shirt outside of a pair of those

multicolor pants so popular at Vineyard cocktail parties.

"May I help you, sir?" Maybe he was a Harvard man. Modulated voice. Very polite. Cold eyes.

"I'd like to see Mr. Sylvia. A business matter. My name is Jackson."

"Does he expect you, sir? He's quite busy in his office."

"Tell him it has to do with Brunner International. Pharmacological division."

His eyes roved over me. I didn't look like anybody from Brunner International, but then I didn't look like anything else in particular, either.

"I'll tell him you're here."

He went down the hall and turned left. I heard him knock on a door. There was a murmur of voices, and then he reappeared and came back down the hall.

"Mr. Sylvia will see you, sir. Follow me, please." Back up the hall we went. At the end of it we turned left and came to a heavy oak door. Leon was kind enough to hold it open for me.

Fred Sylvia was a handsome guy who liked handsome things around him. His wife was handsome, his bodyguard was handsome, and his office was handsome. His desk was carved oak and sported the latest in oversize computers. Fred collected teacups and saucers. They were arranged in rows in a glass-fronted rack on one wall. There was an Oriental carpet on the floor, and what looked to be an early-eighteenth-century painting of a ship hanging in a gold-colored frame on a wall. Fred himself was wearing a white short-sleeved shirt and dark summer trousers. He wore dark boat shoes. He looked like he had just stepped out of *Esquire*. He waved Leon away. Leon left. I shut the door behind him and noticed that it had a lock. I locked it and turned again to Sylvia. I jabbed a thumb at the lock.

"Security. A private talk."

Sylvia's hands were both on his desk. Behind him, French doors opened onto a veranda. "What do you want? You sure as hell don't work for Brunner International. I'll give you five minutes, then out you go."

I walked over to the case of cups and saucers. They were bone china. Exquisitely thin, delicate as butterfly wings. Some looked very old. Nice.

"Five minutes may be enough. You know Billy Martin?"

"The baseball player. No."

"Not the baseball player. A kid here on the island. A few years ago he was pretty strung out on dope. Your boy Danny got him hooked and he stayed hooked for quite a while. Remember?"

"Maybe. My boy's been clean for months. I don't know anything about his ex-friends."

"Well, Billy took the cure and went off to college just like your boy Danny and became really straight arrow. Everybody was proud of him. He went to Brown, his old man's school. He passed all his courses. He was a success story. He'd kicked the habit and become an all-American boy. Only he hadn't. At college he mixed with other users. Grass, coke, and other stuff. Codeine was his specialty. He sold it to other students. There's a lot of money at Brown, and the students can afford expensive habits. The point is that Billy let it slip that his supplier is named Sylvia, and since he's got no contacts off island, it figures that he gets his stuff here. Add everything up and, lo, here I am."

"You're a wacky one, you are. There must be a thousand Sylvias between New Bedford and Nantucket."

"I still have a couple of minutes, Fred—let me use them, okay? Now's here's the point. There's a drug bust brewing, as you no doubt know if you can read, and there is at least one person here on the blessed isle who thinks that maybe Billy Martin was going to fink on his friends and associates in hopes of getting himself a few wide smiles from family and maybe the deity itself."

"I don't know what you're talking about."

"I'm talking about somebody putting a bomb on Billy's boat to keep him from shooting his mouth off."

Sylvia's face did not change, but behind his eyes the gears were turning. Finally he said, "Oh. That boat that blew up. That kid that got killed. He's the one you're talking about."

"No, I'm talking about the one who didn't get killed."

Sylvia shook his head. "My company's boat and captain saved that kid. You think I'd bomb a boat, then save the guy I was trying to kill? I don't think I'd make the ten-most-wanted list if I ran my criminal empire like that. Do you? I think you must have been someplace else when they handed out the brains, Mr. Jackson."

"Maybe your captain didn't know who he was saving. Maybe your right hand doesn't know what your left hand is doing."

"Maybe you're nuts, too. Your time's up. Get out."

"If it wasn't you, who was it? I need a name, Fred." I touched the cabinet holding the china. It, like everything else in the room, was handsome—carved oak, like the door and desk. Maybe Brunner International had an oak forest and gave deals to its middle management. I tugged and felt the cabinet move.

"Time for you to go," said Sylvia. His hand slid under the desk and no doubt touched a button, which Leon no doubt heard. Sylvia looked at me in disgust then with a different expression as I jiggled the china cabinet slightly.

Everyone is afraid of something. Sylvia was afraid of having his china collection destroyed.

"I think I can dump this thing before Leon can get through that door or through those windows or wherever it is he's supposed to appear on the scene. What do you think?"

Sylvia's tongue touched his lips. "Be careful! Those are priceless! Step away!"

"I need a name, Fred. Who wanted Billy Martin dead?"

"I don't know. I tell you, I don't know! Get away from there!"

But instead, I jiggled the cabinet again, a bit harder this time. Sylvia actually went pale.

"Tell me a name."

"I don't know, I don't know!" His voice was higher than before. "For God's sake, don't break any of those pieces. They're irreplaceable! Please, Jackson, be careful!"

"A name."

"I swear to God, Jackson, I don't know a name."

Someone—Leon, no doubt—was pounding on the door.

"That noise makes me nervous," I said. "Tell your man to go away." I rattled the cabinet, and Sylvia screamed at Leon to leave.

"I don't believe you, Mr. Sylvia," I said. "I think you're holding out on me. If I don't get a name, I'm going to start taking these pieces out one at a time and dropping them on the floor, starting right now." And so saying, I opened the cabinet door and took out a tiny cup and saucer, eggshell blue with lines of gold and red entwined in an intricate and subtle design around the rims.

Then Sylvia surprised me. He burst into tears, came racing around from behind his fine desk, and threw himself at me, clutching not at me, but at the cup and saucer in my hand. I let him have them and he pushed at me, trying to get between me and the cabinet. He sobbed and sobbed, cradling the china in one hand and slapping at me with the other. I studied him.

"Okay, Fred, I guess I do believe you after all."

I went to the French windows. As I stepped through to the veranda, I heard his shrill voice: "I'll kill you for this, I'll kill you, I swear I will!"

But I didn't believe that he'd tried to kill Billy or knew who had.

I ran the whole business over in my mind as I drove toward home. As I got to Edgartown, an idea wormed its way up out of my subconscious, or from wherever it is that ideas live before you realize that you have them. I stopped at the police station and asked Helen Viera where the chief was.

"On the street. Where else?"

Where else, indeed? I found him by the paper store.

"Chief," I said, "tell me something. Is it possible that Jim Norris was a narc?"

He looked at me.

"Think about it," I said. "He shows up on the island a couple of years ago. He makes friends with Billy and his family. He's a thirtyish single guy who hangs around where other people his age and a bit younger hang around. People like him. They talk to him, they like him, they get to trust him. But when his work is done and the bust is about to come down, he's supposed to leave town so when the shit hits the fan it won't hit him, too. But suppose somebody caught on to him. Suppose it was Jim who was supposed to get blown up, and not Billy at all? What do you think?"

"I think you're full of shit. I also think you should back away from this. You're getting mixed up with stuff I wouldn't tell you about even if I knew, which I don't."

"You can trust me with your deepest secrets," I said. "I'm a fisherman, and fishermen never pass on stories."

He shook his head in mock astonishment. "As far as I know, Jim Norris was just a beer drinker. I never heard his name mentioned with regard to drugs of any kind."

"But who'd mention it? The users wouldn't because they'd think he was one of them and they wouldn't want to squeal on him. The feds and DEAers wouldn't because they'd know he was one of them, and they wouldn't tell you because maybe they think you local guys are a bunch of stiffs who would blow his cover."

"I read a philosophy book once," said the chief. "It said you can't prove something on the basis of no evidence. You can only prove something on the basis of evidence. Didn't they teach you that sort of thing at the police academy?"

"I don't remember reading any philosophy books at the academy," I said, "but you've got a point."

"Look at this traffic," said the chief. "I'll be glad when Labor Day comes. It gets worse every year, I swear." Then he looked at me. "Go away," he said.

I did.

* 10 *

I went home and ate warmed-over St.-Jacques for lunch while I checked the tide tables. Then I drove to the hospital and went in to see Billy.

"I'm out of here this afternoon," he said with a smile. "They're giving me my walking papers."

I shut the door and sat down. Billy stopped looking happy. I told him everything. From the time his sister came to see me up to the talk I'd just had with the chief. His face went through a number of changes during my narrative. Once or twice he wanted to say something, but I waved him silent. When I was through, I said, "Well, what do you think? Is somebody after you?"

"No. Why should they be?"

I shrugged. "You'd know more about that than I would. According to Julie, you're still dealing. Dealers get hurt; it's an occupational hazard. It happens every day. Somebody gets murdered and in a day or so the police let it out that it was drug related. You're in it for the money, I imagine. And your old man still thinks that you're straight, God help him."

"My old man." His lip curled. "He's got me on such a tight allowance up at school that I can't even have a social life. You're going to tell him, of course."

"Maybe. Is that how you got back into the peddling business? Because you needed more money than your old man was handing out?"

He shrugged. "You know him. He figured he'd spoiled me before so he'd make up for it this time. I was always broke."

I doubted that Billy had been as poor as he claimed, but then one man's poverty is another's riches. If you feel poor, maybe you are. On the other hand, maybe Billy just liked dealing dope. Maybe he just liked the life-style or the power it gave him over the people who paid for his product.

"Where'd you get the stuff you sold, Billy?"

His eyes wandered away and his mouth tightened. Did Billy have a code of honor? Would he refuse to rat on his own supplier? Yes, he would. "I won't tell you that," he said.

"Your sister thinks that somebody tried to kill you. Your dealer might be a likely choice if the word got around that you were about to become an informer."

"No. The people I used to know weren't that sort."

"How about the people you still know?"

"No. Besides, I'm not informing on anybody."

I am not a theater critic, so I don't always know an act when I see one. Billy's voice was a bit cracked, and the muscles at the hinges of his jaw were working. I changed course.

"So nobody would want to kill you. You were close to Jim Norris. Would anybody want to kill him?"

Billy looked startled. "Jim? What do you mean?"

"I mean maybe somebody was after him, and not you. Maybe the right guy got blown up after all."

Big eyes. "What are you talking about?" Billy was sitting up.

"I mean maybe Jim was a narc, an undercover operator for the state or feds. Maybe somebody got on to him and got rid of him before he could testify. Do you know if he had any enemies, anybody who might want to kill him?"

"No."

"Do you think he was a narc?"

The shock was past him. Billy settled back on the pillow again. "No, I don't think so. I suppose he could have been, but . . . He would have told me, I think. We were almost like brothers, you know. We didn't hit it off when he first came here, but in the end we really got along. Hey, do you have to tell my family all this? Look, I admit it—I peddled some stuff at college because I needed more money than my dad was sending me. It wasn't much, just some grass I had stashed and some codeine. I'm really not a pusher, I swear."

I looked at him, wishing I could see into his soul.

"Hey," he said, "I'll stop. I'll get rid of the stuff I have left. I swear it. Look, you can come with me when I get out this afternoon and you can watch me burn it, or whatever. That's it—you come and watch me. What do you say? Please . . . don't tell my family."

"You'll need somebody to drive you home," I said. "I'll do it. Then you give me your stash and I'll get rid of it. Everything you have."

"Okay, okay. It's a deal. I'll really go straight this time, I swear. Just don't tell my family."

Bad habits are hard to break. I considered myself and my corncob pipe and did not feel particularly superior to Billy and others whose addictions sometimes dominate their lives.

I went to see George. Susie was there. George looked pretty good, I thought. He was getting some color back.

We exchanged insults. When I left, I gave Susie a nod and she followed me out into the hall.

"As far as I can tell," I said, "nobody is after Billy. I've spent three days asking questions and there's not a hint anywhere that anybody was after Billy. It looks like it was just an accident."

"No." Her jaw was firmer than her brother's. "There was nothing wrong with the boat when I took it out. It was perfect."

"Things can go wrong. They don't stay perfect."

Tears were suddenly oozing from her eyes and running down her face. "The worst part is that maybe it was my fault. I told Jim that I loved him and I think I drove him away. If I hadn't said it, maybe he'd have stayed on the island and then he wouldn't have been out in that boat."

"Cut it out, Susie. You'll be guilty of plenty of things in your life before you're through. Don't try to be guilty of this, because you're not."

She crossed her arms and looked down at the floor. "It was Saturday. He had the day off. We were messing around on the beach with a Frisbee and we were really happy and I just ran up to him and told him I loved him. And I tried to kiss him, but he pulled away. He looked shocked, like he was almost sick, and he said, 'No. No, you don't. Not like that.' And he backed away. Then he shook his head and walked off. That afternoon he told Dad that he was leaving the island and going home. I must have cried for hours. When Billy found me in my room that evening and I told him about it, he was furious. He said he'd find out about it and he went to find Jim. But when he talked to me the next day, he wasn't mad anymore, and he and Jim were still friends and planning that last fishing trip. So it was my fault, you see."

"No," I said, "it wasn't your fault. It was just one of those things. People fall in love with people who don't love them back, that's all. I know he liked you—he just didn't love you the way you loved him." I was trying to remember the way it was to be sixteen and in love and was glad I was past that. Then I remembered Zee and wasn't sure I was past it at all. I dug out my handkerchief, glad that it was a clean one. "Here."

She dabbed at her eyes and blew her nose. The Martins were all going through hard times.

"Call your mom and tell her that I'm bringing Billy home, then go back and visit your dad." She nodded, still looking down, and gave me my handkerchief. "It wasn't your fault," I said again, trying not to sound forlorn.

I went along the hall to emergency and found Zee. She looked very fine.

"I'm going down the beach about seven-thirty," I said. "Want to come along? There'll be pretty good light until after nine."

No hesitation. "I'll meet you in the Katama parking lot. You still have my rod and gear."

"Oh, goll darn. I forgot to give them back to you."

"Sure," she said, "and I forgot to pick them up last night." She had wonderful teeth.

Feeling good, I went back to Billy's room. Someone had brought him clean clothes and I helped him get into them. He had a lot of tender places and still wore bandages. But he could walk, so we checked him out and got into the Landcruiser.

In the five years I'd known the Martins, Billy had treated everyone else badly at one time or another, but had shown only affection for Susie. Was being mad at a man who had refused his sister's love enough motive to make Billy a murderer?

I asked him.

He gave me a shocked look. "What? Me? Are you crazy? Jesus Christ!"

"Susie says you were really mad. I know how you feel about her."

He stared out of the windshield, breathing hard. We drove past the rows of cars that lined the road beside the beach. "All right, I admit I was mad. Nobody hurts my sister, you know? I found him up at the Fireside and I was still hot, but we didn't fight, we talked. And he told me she was his sister, that she was like a sister to him, and that he didn't know how to handle the way she felt and so he was going to go back home out west. He'd been all over, you know. Said he had an itchy foot and it was time to go home and settle down and let Susie find somebody who'd be right for her. Anyway, we had a couple of beers and we decided to go fishing in the boat." Then his fists clenched. "We were friends. I hadn't liked him too much when he first started hanging out with Dad, but it turned out he was a good guy."

When we got to the Martin place, his mother met him with tears and tried to put him right to bed, but he put her off.

"I've been in bed for days, Mom. I'm fine. J.W. and I are going to walk for a while so I can get some of the kinks out. Don't worry, we're not going far. I just want to get some air, you know?"

We strolled out to the barn where George kept his decoys, his fishing gear, and the flat-bottomed skiff he used for duck hunting and scalloping. We climbed a ladder to the loft and Billy moved some boards and buckets aside and got out a nylon athletic bag. Inside were several vials of clear liquid, a pack of white powder, and about a kilo of green leaves packaged in small bags.

"That's it," said Billy. "That's the whole stash. I should have gotten rid of it long ago, but . . ."

I still had my pipes. I closed the bag and we left the barn. I put the bag in the Landcruiser.

"Thanks," said Billy. "Thanks for helping."

"Go see your mother," I said. "She's probably got a bowl of chicken soup for you."

He went in and I went home, wondering what I'd say if some cop stopped me and asked me what was in the bag. At home I got Julie's stuff and added it to the bag and put the bag out in the storage shed in more or less plain sight. The purloined letter ploy. I wasn't sure what I wanted to do with the stuff. Until I did decide, I had quite a stash of my own.

It seemed that I was at a dead end in my investigations, such as they were. I had a beer, then worked in the garden for a while. Greens were popping up more and more every day. My lettuce looked promising. I could taste a fresh imaginary salad in my mouth. After an hour I went in and cleaned the house. I changed the sheets and vacuumed with the vacuum cleaner I'd salvaged from the dump. In Edgartown, people throw away things you wouldn't believe. When I was through inside, I mowed the lawn with the lawnmower I'd salvaged from the dump. The place looked pretty good.

I thought of Zee while I took a shower. I have an indoor winter shower and an outdoor summer shower. The outdoor one is twice as good, and I used that. I felt half

good, half discontented. I had another beer and heated up
the last of the stuffed bluefish for supper. Delicious.

At seven I drove down to Katama and waited. The last
of the beachers were going home after a long day in the
Vineyard sun. The waves rolled in, and four-by-fours
came off the beach as others came down the highway and
turned off through the sand toward Wasque. At seven-
thirty Zee's Jeep pulled up alongside of the Landcruiser.
She got out, locked up, and climbed in beside me. She
wore jeans and a sweatshirt and her hair was wrapped in a
kerchief.

We went down to the beach.

There were a couple of dozen four-by-fours down at the
point. I stopped at the right-hand end of the line. I kicked
off my sandals and Zee climbed into her waders and we
went to work. Her casts were straight and getting longer.
I caught fish and she didn't. She didn't give up, though.
After a while, I went over to her.

She had a disgusted look on her face. "I can't get out to
them. They're beyond my cast. I can't throw half as far as
you and the rest of these guys."

"You're doing fine. Try my rod. It's graphite. The latest
thing. Its action is different from yours, but once you get
it down you'll add several yards to your cast."

"But what'll you use?"

"Here. Just try it."

"All right."

She threw the plug straight up the first time and into the
surf at her feet the next.

"Great, huh?" She laughed, shaking her head.

Using her rod, I made three casts. On the third, about
two turns of the reel in, the rod bent. I set the hook and

turned to her. "This is your fish. You want to bring him in?"

"Bring in your own fish, Jefferson!" She was getting the feel of the graphite. I landed my fish and watched her as I took the plug out of its mouth.

When she finally made the cast correctly, I could see it from the start. The rod came back, swept forward and snapped the plug in a long, high flight that arched far out into the chop. The plug hit the water and the fish hit the plug and the rod bent. Zee hauled back and somebody yelled, "Yee haw!" It was me. I started to run down to help her, then stopped myself. I could hear the reel sing. She had a good one.

She fought the fish for five minutes before she gained much on it. She would stop and reel it in only to have it run off again with the line. Had I set the drag too light? I didn't think so. She worked the rod and finally began to gain. The rushes away from shore were shorter. Then they stopped and she was getting him in. Fifty feet out, the fish came dancing out of the water, standing on its tail.

"A beauty!" It was me again.

She brought it into the surf and backed up, the rod bent in a lovely arc. I ran down then, and as the fish flopped up onto the sand, I got between it and the waves. Many a fish has been lost right there. They give a last toss of their heads and they're back in the surf and gone. Zee wasn't going to lose this one.

Come on down and get him, I thought. Keep the line tight. She reeled down, leaned, and got a hand in his gills and pulled the fish up to the Landcruiser. Her cheeks were bright and she was wet with sweat. She was laughing and panting.

"Whee Hawkin!" She jammed the rod into the spike on

the front bumper, took the pliers from the hood, and got her plug back. "Wow! I am wiped out!"

I got the scales and weighed her catch. "A thirteen-pounder. Not bad, pardner."

She grinned and I grinned. I slapped her on the shoulder. She patted the graphite. "Now I know the secret of your success. All this time I thought it was skill."

"Damn," I said. "There goes my image."

We fished for another hour, until it was too dark to see the plugs hit the water. I felt good and we laughed a lot. She got three more fish, but none as big as the first one. On the way back, we scaled them at the Herring Creek and she gave all but the big fish to me.

"I'm keeping this one," she said. "I'll eat it for the next month. I won't have to buy food until July!" I liked her for being proud and happy. "Come and help me eat it," she said. "Tomorrow night?"

"Yes."

* 11 *

When I got home, I filleted the fish and put the fillets in the fridge in a pan of water mixed with sugar and salt. The next morning I washed them off and set them on racks to air-dry for an hour. It was smoking day.

My smoker is out behind the shed. I made it from an old freezer I got from the dump and a 220-volt system I got from a stove there. I smolder hickory chips in an old frying pan for about six hours to get the fillets the way I like them. I bow to no one when it comes to smoked bluefish.

When the fish were in the smoker and smoke was oozing out from around the door at the approved rate, I sat down by the phone. Why was I doing that? I was going to have the biggest phone bill in the history of the world. I phoned Quinn. He was out, but someone answered his phone at the *Globe*. I left a message: Jackson wants to know if the names Billy Martin or Jim Norris mean anything to anybody. Cryptic stuff. The guy who took the message didn't even seem curious.

I looked at my watch. Eight A.M. Oregon was three hours earlier. Five A.M. there. Too early. I got out my newspaper clipping and again read the names of Jim Norris's parents:

Mr. and Mrs. Bradley Norris. They had two other children, a daughter, Nancy, and a son, Bradley, Jr. I dialed 1-503-555-1212 and got their telephone number.

At ten o'clock Quinn called. Neither name I'd left was in his notes, but both were now.

"What are you doing, J.W.? I thought you were out of the fuzz business?"

"I don't know what I'm doing."

"Ah-ha! So you're in the newspaper business."

"I admit to being a sorry sort of guy, but I haven't sunk that low yet."

"You're pretty insulting for a man who's about to get a hot piece of genuine rumor."

My ears perked up. "Not just a rumor, but a genuine rumor?"

"A genuine one. From what we in the fourth estate refer to as a 'reliable source.'"

"Let's have it."

"It'll cost you. I want a bluefish on my line before the season passes. And I want you to smoke it for me so I can bring it home to my mother. She loves the stuff."

"You got it. What's the rumor?"

"The rumor is that five days from now a lot of heavy DEA people plus a number of state narcs will be arriving on your quiet little island to perform a law enforcement operation that very night. If I can talk my editor into it, I'll be down myself to cover the story."

"Well, for God's sake, stay out of sight. If the news gets out that a big-time media guy like yourself has arrived on the Vineyard, the baddies will know that something is about to happen and they'll head for the hills."

"I'll wear Groucho glasses and mustache. They'll never

recognize me till it's too late. The next day I'll expect fishing trip."

"You'll get it."

I put more chips in the smoker. The fillets were stil pale and wet. Fishing takes patience. Smoking fish take more patience. Lots of things take patience. I felt a littl twinge near my spine where the bullet still rested. Was i working closer to the nerves or farther away? Or was i staying put, just like the doctors said it probably would The spine, with all its parts, nerves, and blood vessels i not one of God's best designs. It's pretty fragile for the amount of work it's supposed to do. I hadn't even hur when it happened. I hadn't even known I was shot. Too much was going on at the time. I'd been shooting, too and the guy who shot me was falling down about the same time I was. I only hurt later. Now, after five years, only had a twinge occasionally and the knowledge that the bullet they decided not to try to take out might one day move a bit.

At noon the fillets were browning nicely and I tele-phoned Jim Norris's parents. His mother answered. She was calm. I introduced myself as a friend of Jim's.

"Yes," she said. "He was the sort of person who made friends wherever he went."

"We fished together," I said. "He was a nice guy. I want to ask you some questions about him. I hope you don't mind."

"I don't mind. The funeral was yesterday. It was a closed-casket ceremony. They said it was better that way, so that's the way we did it. It's better to remember him the way he was, don't you think?"

"Yes." I recognized the numbness of feeling that lay

behind her calm. Nothing could be worse than losing a child. "Tell me, Mrs. Norris, did Jim ever say why he came to Martha's Vineyard? Was there any particular reason?"

"Oh, no. Jimmy traveled around everywhere. He said he had a sugar foot, you know. After the army, he didn't want to stay home, so he'd just go off and work. He liked people and he liked seeing the country. He'd work somewhere and then come back home for a while and then leave again. Why, I guess he must have been all over the United States. He was a carpenter and he could get a job just about anywhere. I suppose he just wanted to live on an island for a while."

"Did he tell you anything about what he was doing here? Any people he met?"

"I have his letters. He wrote every week. He was very good about that. He did mention his friends, of course. The only names I remember right at this moment are in one family. I think the father's name was George and the children were Bill and Susan. I can't recall the last name. He didn't use last names much, just first ones. I know he was excited about knowing them and that he was happy when he was with them."

"Did he ever tell you about why, in particular, he decided to come to the island?"

"Why, no. I remember he was down in Georgia working when he wrote that he was going up there. He was really sort of excited about it, I remember. I don't think he'd ever been in New England before and he was anxious to go up there. That was so much like him—he was always excited to go someplace new. We just got a card that he was coming home, you know. I imagine he must have mailed it just the day before he was killed. It arrived after we got the news. . . ." Her voice faded, grew thin like dispersing fog.

"Mrs. Norris, is your husband home? May I speak to him?"

"What? Oh, no, he's not. Brad's at work. He thought that it might be better if he just went to work as usual. He said that life goes on, that it was better if he just went to work and did something. I think he was right, don't you? Things do go on, of course. The lawn, the dishes, the bills. Everything just keeps happening and we have to do the same things we always do. I don't know. . . ."

"Mrs. Norris, please, was Jim closer to his sister or his brother?"

"Oh, to Nancy. Young Braddy is much younger, you know . . ."

"May I speak to Nancy, please?"

"Of course. Now, let me see . . . No, no, I'm sorry. I think . . . yes, Nancy's out, too. She's gone down for the mail. It's such a nice day. . . ."

"Please have her call me collect when she gets in. Do you have a pencil and paper handy?"

"Oh . . . yes, of course."

I gave her my number and had her read it back to me. When she'd done that, I said, "I'm sorry about Jim, Mrs. Norris. Please accept my sympathies."

"Thank you," she said in her dull voice.

I put on an Emmy Lou tape and made lunch while Emmy Lou sang of the pangs of love. A hunk of cheese, a slab of white bread, chutney, and a fresh salad, washed down with beer. I checked on the smoker and added more wood chips. The fish were beginning to glaze. As I came in, the phone rang. It was Nancy Norris. I thanked her for calling and said: "I don't want you to be more unhappy than you already are, but you should know that there is a remote possibility that the explosion that killed your brother was not accidental. I didn't want to tell your mother, but I must tell you because I need information about Jim."

"What are you talking about? What do you mean it wasn't an accident? Do you mean somebody killed him on purpose? What do you mean? Are you a policeman?"

"I'm a friend of Jim's and of his friends the Martins, the people who owned the boat. It's possible that the explosion wasn't just an accident. I'm just trying to find out everything I can, you understand? May I speak plainly?"

"Plainly? Yes, of course. I want you to."

I told her about Billy's past and about my failure to find anything to substantiate Susie's suspicion that someone had tried to kill her brother. "And now," I said, "I'm trying to check Jim out. Jim was a friend of Billy's and so maybe Jim knew the same dealers and distributors on the island that Billy knew. Maybe Jim was a user, too. Was he? I need to know."

"My God," said her voice, "this is unreal."

"Was he a user? Did he smoke or shoot up? Was he on pills?"

"No. Yes. I mean, is there anyone Jimmy's age who hasn't tried grass? But no more. No, he was a beer drinker. We used to call him 'Red Neck' he was so straight. He told me once that he couldn't work stoned, that it wasn't his thing."

"Did he ever work with law enforcement agencies?"

"What do you mean? As a cop? No, never. He was a carpenter. He liked working with wood, with his hands. He was smart, but he never wanted to go to college or anything. He could always find work wherever he went. Why did you ask that?"

"If he wasn't a user, I thought maybe he was an undercover cop."

"Well, wouldn't the cops say so, if he was?"

"Yes. But sometimes one agency doesn't give information to another one. The feds keep secrets from the state cops; the state cops keep information from the locals; that sort of thing. I guess you're right that if he was a cop some agency would have announced it by now. It was a dumb question for me to have asked you." I had no more even semi-logical questions to ask her, but I needed to grope around some more. Something wouldn't let me let it go. "Did he ever mention any enemies? Did he ever mention anybody he perhaps argued with?"

"No. Never. Not ever—really. I mean, he wrote home a lot and even kept a journal that he'd bring home when he came and he'd let us read it. He was funny and interesting in the way he looked at things and the stuff he wrote about. I never remember him writing or talking about arguments or fights. He liked people and they liked him."

"Did he get along with your parents? Was there ever any strain between them?"

"No! They wanted him home more, but they loved him and he loved them. Not even natural parents could be better. None of us could love our natural parents more or be loved more. It's so sad; my dad and mom are in shock, I think. All of us are. . . ."

"You're adopted children, then? The Norrises aren't your natural parents?"

"No. They couldn't have children, so they took us in as foster children and then adopted us."

"They never tried to keep it from you?"

"Oh, no. They told us when we were very young. They got us when we were babies and told us as soon as we could understand. They told us how our real parents loved us but couldn't keep us and so Mom and Dad got to have us like gifts from God. They're the best parents in the world."

"I'm sure."

"When we asked questions about our real parents, they always told us as much as they knew. All three of us kids had different parents, you know. None of us are blood brothers or sister. I'm a Billings, Brad's a Hogan, and Jim—Jim was a Singleton."

"Those were . . . ?"

"Our mothers' names. We each got our mother's name as our middle name, so we'd always have a link with our blood kin. I'm Nancy Billings Norris."

"That was a good thing for your folks to have done for you."

"Yes. It's not good to keep the truth from children. Mom understood that. She's a nurse, you know, and she knew our mothers when they were in the hospital. She understood what it meant to be a mother. She still works there. She's good with patients. The doctors just love her. . . ."

"I'm sure."

"I don't know my real father, but that's only because Mom never knew his name. My natural mother never told Mom, I guess. But Mom would tell me, if she knew." Nancy talked and talked, and I was unable not to listen because I owed it to her to let her keep talking. She told me about Brad and Mom and Dad and Jim and then abruptly stopped. "I'm sorry," she said. "I'm babbling. . . ."

Some people talk, some people cry. Grief shows itself in many forms.

"I appreciate your help," I said. "Thank you for your time."

"Do you really think that it might not have been an accident? That somebody might have. . . ?"

"Susie Martin and the guy at the boatyard both swear that the boat was fine when the boys took it out. That's the only reason anyone could have for thinking the explosion was deliberately caused. But accidents happen, and so far I haven't any reason to think this wasn't just exactly that. I just had to check loose ends, you understand. If you think of anything else, please call me collect. If I can help you in return, please let me know."

"Thanks. We'll be all right. Eventually."

I hung up and got a beer and went outside and sat in the sun. People pay thousands of dollars to loll around drinking beer on Martha's Vineyard and I could do it for nothing. My tan was immature; it needed work. Fearless of skin cancer, I drank my beer and thought things over. When the beer was gone, I got another. It was a good beer-drinking day—hot and dry. Not much moisture in the air. I turned on the garden sprinkler and watched the arc of spray sweep back and forth, making little rainbows.

When my second beer was gone, I went out back, turned off the smoker, and carried the racks of fish to the screened porch for cooling. The fillets were brownish bronze and shiny. Unable to wait, I got out some cream cheese and red onion and had these plus smoked bluefish on a broiled bagel. Paradise enow! When the rest of the fillets were cool, I wrapped them in plastic wrap and put them in the fridge. I never get tired of smoked bluefish. I use it in omelets, salads, snacks, and casseroles, and I like it any time of day. Could it be that God is a cosmic bluefish whose essence is manifest in each of the particular fish I eat? It seems possible.

* 12 *

"What's this?" asked Zee as I stepped through the door.

"Sauterne, crackers, and smoked bluefish pâté." I handed her the paper bag. "There's some just plain smoked bluefish in there, too. If you don't like it, we can still be friends, but our relationship will be under a considerable strain."

"Love me, love my smoked bluefish?"

"I might make an exception in your case."

Her house was small, but neat. Three or four rooms, I guessed. I could see into the kitchen. A table was set there, complete with candles. The living room was furnished with a couch, coffee table, two comfortable-looking chairs, a bookcase of paperbacks and a baby TV set. There was a worn rug on the floor. I couldn't tell whether it was Navaho, Mexican, Eastern, or African. A lot of designs look alike.

Zee poured us wine and set out the crackers and pâté on a plate on the coffee table. She put some pâté on a cracker. I watched her.

"I hope I like this," she said.

"If you don't, lie about it."

She sniffed at it and ate it. Her eyes lit up and she dug

in for more. "Jefferson, I'm not sure I want to feed you. I don't know if my food is up to your standards."

"I was brought up to have absolute faith in nurses."

"A good point. Your mother raised you with a proper sense of values. Are you supposed to be eating that stuff so fast?"

"I know I'm supposed to smile modestly when I make something good, but I'm the first to praise my work. This stuff has no staying power when I'm around. It disappears."

"You can say that again! I thought you brought this up to impress me with your culinary genius. But to do that, you've got to leave some for me!"

"Slow eaters deserve what they don't get," I said. "But since it's you . . ."

She was wearing jeans and a checked shirt, and I could smell a faint musky perfume when she sat beside me on the couch. I felt good. We drank wine and ate all of the pâté.

"What's in this, Jefferson? Or do you keep your recipes secret?"

"Crumbled smoked bluefish, chopped onion, a dash of horseradish, and cream cheese. I use that soft onion-flavored kind you can buy. Mix it up and there you are. It's a recipe passed down through my family for generations. You're the first outsider who's ever learned it, but I know I can trust you with the secret."

"Because I'm a nurse."

"Absolutely."

She poured more wine. "And what are you?"

"I'm not anything," I said. "I'm sort of retired."

"You're a fisherman," she said. "You have a commercial

shellfish license and you make money scalloping in the fall and winter and clamming in the summer."

"That's true. I also sell bluefish. Who told you?"

"George. I asked him about you. He told me all about you."

"Only the good stuff, I hope." In five years, friends tell each other a lot even if they never planned to.

"He told me that you were a policeman in Boston and that you got shot and that you retired with a pension because there's a bullet lodged near your spine."

"It went in my front," I said. "I've had two belly buttons for six years now. The extra one is the only flaw in my otherwise perfect physique."

"Wrong," said Zee. "I've seen your legs, remember? George says those scars are from Vietnam."

"Shrapnel," I said. "Vintage 1972. It's almost all out now, but it ended my early hopes of becoming a model for Bermuda shorts."

"You seem to have a habit of standing in front of flying pieces of metal. That explains why I almost got you with my fishing plug the morning we met. I knew it couldn't really be my fault."

"Are you practicing every spare moment so I'll be impressed the next time we go fishing?"

"Of course. Now I want you to tell me about yourself. If we're going to be friends, I want to know about you."

"I want to know about you, too," I said. "So far, all I know is where you live, what you do for money, and how you fish."

She got up. "I'm putting supper in the oven. After you eat, you'll also know how I cook."

Broiled bluefish with a butter-lemon-dill sauce, baby

peas, and wild rice; a light but rich flan for dessert. Coffee and Cognac afterward. Yum to the third power!

"All right," I said with a sigh, "I accept your proposal. We'll get married in the morning."

"Fate is cruel," she said with sort of a smile. "I'm already married." She looked into her brandy snifter and then took a sip.

"That's what the guy says the next morning," I said, recovering nicely. "I couldn't imagine you not being married unless you just liked other women."

"He's a doctor now," she said. "The familiar tale of the young wife earning the bread while her man goes through medical school and then being told that she's no longer his type. The divorce will be final in a couple of months."

"My blue moon has turned to gold again," I said, finding a big smile on my face. Her answering smile was rather small and crooked. "Since it's confession time," I said, "I was married once, too. But first there was Nam and then there was my being a cop and she was under more strain than probably any woman should have to stand. Never knowing if I was going to come home, she said. She's married to a teacher up in Boston now. Nice guy. She's happy. We're still friends. Your ex may be a doctor, but take my word for it—he's a jerk, too."

"Yes, he is!" She grinned. Then, "Tell me about your family."

"I'm it. My mother died when I was very young. I don't remember much about her. My father's been dead for ten years. He was the kind who only got married once. I have an older sister who lives in New Mexico with her family. I see her every few years. We get along."

We watched the news on the tube. The Sox lost again.

"The dumbest team in baseball," I said. "Great outfield, but they never have pitching."

"Their pitchers are okay," said Zee. "The guys are young, but they can throw. They've got no middle to their infield, that's their problem. The pitchers get killed because ground balls get by the shortstop and second baseman all the time."

"Naw. Check the stats. Our shortstop and second baseman don't make any more errors than anybody else's. It's the pitchers. No consistency."

"They don't make errors because they can't get to the ball. You don't get errors on balls you don't reach. They'll be lucky to finish fifth in the East."

"They can hit, though."

"D," said Zee. "You win with D. No D, no pennant."

"They play softball in Oak Bluffs on Sundays," I said. "You want to go?"

"Sure," said Zee.

"I remember being a teenager and taking girls I was scared of to the movies. I was afraid to touch them, so I'd use the old yawn-and-stretch ploy and end up with my arm across their shoulders. If they put up with it, I got braver. If they didn't, I felt terrible. I'm thinking of trying it now, but I'm nervous."

We were sitting on her couch. The late show was fluttering at us. Zee looked at me. "Well?"

"Well what?"

"Well, are you going to try it or not?"

"Well, yes."

I did. She put up with it. I got braver. When we kissed, her lips were moist and there was hunger in them. We were both a bit breathless when we parted.

"Definitely more than a postpubescent kiss." I said. "If you'd done that to me when I was fifteen, I'd have probably split my pants on the spot."

She glanced down and laughed. "You're not doing so badly right now."

I went home about midnight, feeling good about everything but leaving.

On Sunday we went to the game and then down to the Fireside for beer. The place was jumping, as usual, and the crowd made us feel like senior citizens. The music from the machine was rock. Bonzo saw us at the bar and came over.

"Hey, J.W., how you doing?" He smiled his sweet, vacant smile. I introduced him to Zee, and he bobbed his head and smiled even more. "Pleased to meet you, I'm sure. Hey, J.W., we going to go fishing again?"

"Sure, Bonzo." I turned to Zee. "You work tomorrow, right?"

"Right."

"Okay, Bonzo. How about tomorrow?"

Bonzo's simple face lit up. "Hey, great, J.W.! That's great! You got a pole for me, like last time?"

"Sure." I ran the tides through my mind. "You be here at ten o'clock tomorrow morning, okay? I'll pick you up."

"Hey," said Bonzo. "Thanks." Then he looked thoughtfully at Zee and me, frowned, smiled, said, "So long, you two," and walked off with his broom.

"Bad acid," I said to Zee. "They say he used to be a really smart kid. He was a member of the pack Billy used to run with, I'm told." Zee drank her beer. "He's okay," I said. "He likes birds. He's got a tape recorder and a mike and he likes to go out and try to record bird songs. I take him fishing sometimes."

"You're okay, too, Jefferson," said Zee.

"You, too, Zee. I like a woman who can cook and hold down a steady job."

She whacked me in the ribs with her elbow.

Monday was bright and blue. A Chamber of Commerce day. The June People were all over the beach well before noon. I picked up Bonzo and we headed for Wasque. Bonzo had his tape recorder. At the edge of the tern nesting ground just before Wasque, he had me stop.

"I'm gonna get me some songs," he said. He took his tape recorder over to a low dune and placed it in the sand. He put a mike on the end of a stick. "My tape runs for an hour," he said, smiling. "I bet I get some good songs this time."

"Somebody may just come along and take your machine," I said.

He gave me a sly smile. "No. Look." He took out a neatly lettered paper enclosed in cellophane and thumbtacked it to the stick. It said: ORNITHOLOGICAL RESEARCH. DO NOT DISTURB. Bonzo tapped a finger to his temple. "I'm no fool, you know. I always put this up. People leave my things alone. They don't want to get into trouble with a scientist."

"Pretty smart, Bonzo."

"You're a fisherman," said Bonzo, smiling. "I'm an ornithologist. You're smart about fish and I'm smart about birds." He blinked his lashes over his hollow eyes. "I like birds best. That's okay with you, isn't it? You don't mind my liking birds best, do you, J.W.?"

"Naw," I said. "Birds sound better than fish every time. And fish can't fly."

"Flying fish can!" His laugh was like a child's. "I got you

there, J.W., didn't I? Come on, admit it, I got you on that one! Flying fish!"

I felt a grin on my face. "Yeah, you got me, Bonzo. Come on, let's try for a bluefish." We got into the Land-cruiser and drove to the point. I wondered what Bonzo might have become if he'd stuck to drinking beer.

He fished like a young boy, casting tirelessly and largely in vain, but never stopping. There was an awkwardness about him that kept him from ever getting any better, but he loved being there in the sun, feeling the wind in his face and the sand under his bare feet, seeing the blue ocean reaching out to the southern horizon. And he kept his mind on his business, never stopping to play with the water that surged up and down the sloping beach after every wave broke, but standing solid in the swirling water and keeping an intent, vacant eye on his plug as he tossed it out and reeled it in. He was happy for me when I finally tied into a fish far out at the end of my cast and got the rascal in after he did some tail dancing and short runs along the wave tops. And he was happy every time I caught a fish after that. And I was happy when at last the fish moved in closer and he could reach them with his short cast and he got one and landed it.

His smile reached his ears. He took the fish to the Landcruiser and carefully removed the plug, using my long-nosed pliers. Bluefish have teeth like little razors. Bonzo had once tried to retrieve a half-swallowed plug with his fingers and had lost some blood in the process. After that, he always used the pliers. I had a couple of scarred fingers myself. Bluefish don't care who they chew.

The fish were there for about an hour, and then they

went off to wherever it is that bluefish go when they're tired of being caught. Bonzo and I had beer and smoked bluefish salad sandwiches for lunch, then went and got his tape recorder and mike. On the way home he played his tape for me. I heard the hush of wind, the sound of engines as four-by-fours went by, and faintly, very faintly, the occasional cheep of a bird. Bonzo beamed.

"You hear that, J.W.? Those are terns. I like terns."

"I like terns, too," I said. "I like snowy egrets better and I like oyster catchers even better."

"And blue herons," said Bonzo, nodding, "and ospreys and pheasants."

"And pheasants," I agreed, thinking of hunting season, "and Canada geese . . ."

"And swans and black ducks . . ."

By the time I got Bonzo home, we must have gone through every bird on Martha's Vineyard. That is, Bonzo went through them. My bird lore runs thin. He rattled off names like a living Peterson guidebook.

Bonzo lived near the Oak Bluffs Camp Meeting grounds in a neat gingerbread house with pink and blue shutters. Pink and blue flowers grew in pink and blue pots on the porch. His mother had her colors down pat. She came out when we stopped in front of the house. Bonzo showed her his fish and turned on his tape recorder. His mother smiled and patted his shoulder and told him to go fillet the fish. Then she smiled at me. She taught math at the regional high school and her son Bonzo had been and probably always would be her joy and burden.

"Thank you, J.W. It was kind of you."

"We had a good time. Do you have enough fish? I've got several more in back."

"No. There's only the two of us. But thanks."

I sold the fish at the market. The price was still pretty good. I used my profit to buy gas and replenish my dwindling beer supply. In case someone bombed the liquor store I liked to have survival rations.

* 13 *

It was midafternoon when I got home. When I turned off the engine I heard the phone ringing. I got to it. It was Nancy Norris.

"Something's happened," she said. "Maybe you can help."

"If I can."

"They've shipped Jimmy's things home. His clothes and his tools and all. But they didn't send his ring or his journal. I talked to the mortuary here because I thought he might have been wearing it. . . . It was a closed casket service, you know. . . ."

"Yes."

"But they said he wasn't wearing it. I asked them if— They said his hands were not hurt very much, but that there wasn't any ring. I know he probably just lost it somewhere in his travels, but he never said so in his letters and he would have told us, I think, because it was really the only thing of his mother's, the only thing he got from her. He always wore it. My mom is so upset. . . . And we especially wanted his journal. You know, so we'd know what he'd been doing and thinking during those last days. . . . But it's not with his books. Can you . . . could you look for them? It would mean a lot to my folks and me, too. I . . ."

"Maybe he kept the book under his mattress or somewhere. Maybe they missed it when they collected his things. Maybe the coroner took the ring off during his examination and forgot about it. I'll be glad to look around."

"The ring wasn't valuable, but it means a lot to us. It's just one of those high school class rings that you can buy when you graduate. It's gold looking and it has a red stone in it and it says Longview High School 1951. It was his mother's. She died giving birth and Mom got it when she got Jimmy. She gave it to him before he was even big enough to wear it. He used to hang it on a chain around his neck until he was big enough to wear it on his finger. I really appreciate your help, Mr. Jackson."

"I'll ask around. Can I do anything else for you?"

I couldn't. We rang off and I brought in the beer from the Landcruiser and popped one. I was giving serious thought to whipping up some smoked bluefish pâté and piling it on crackers for a snack, when I heard a car coming down my driveway. I looked out over the open half of the Dutch door and saw a large black Caddy pull into the yard. The door opened and Leon got out. I waited to see if he had company, but he did not. I knew why he had come and went out to meet him.

"I'll get right to the point," he said as I came outside. "Mr. Sylvia was very annoyed with the way you threatened him. He wants to make sure it never happens again. My job is to protect Mr. Sylvia or, having failed that, as indeed I failed when you visited him, to extract suffering proportionate to that which he suffered."

"What do you have in mind?"

"I've been instructed to break you up a bit. Nothing fatal, I assure you, but it will be painful and probably will debilitate you for a few days or weeks. I recommend no resistance, since such would require me to use more force than otherwise."

"You're very literate," I said.

"Very intelligent, too," said Leon, "and very strong and fast. I played professional football for three years and earned enough money to begin medical school. My medical training has taught me a good deal about how to damage the human body. I know pretty well what to do and how to do it. I think we should get started. Please keep in mind that I can outrun you, outmuscle you, and probably outthink you. You are going to experience some pain, but you will recover from it if you don't force me to go to extremes."

"How many more years of medical school do you have left?"

"I'm in my second year."

"Well, Leon, before we begin the games, I have a word to say. While I haven't the slightest doubt that you can probably outrun and outmuscle me, I'm not sure you can beat me up without risk. I'd guess, for example, that you probably left football for the same reason most young players do—injury. And since the most famous and career-ending injuries are knee injuries, I'd guess that that's the sort that you suffered. And I assure you that if you insist on trying to maim me, I will concentrate my energies on smashing one or both of your knees. I hope I make myself clear." Leon looked thoughtful. "You should also know that I do have some training, and even though I'm growing old and gray, I've not forgotten it."

"I have my duty, nevertheless," said Leon.

"Your duty is to gain guarantees that I'll never again discomfort Sylvia. You have my personal assurance that I'll never again enter the house. I never expect to see him again, for that matter. On the other hand, if you succeed in breaking me up, I'll someday mend, and being the kind of guy I am, I will no doubt take out my irritation on him in person."

"Mr. Sylvia wants revenge as well as guarantees."

"My recommendation is that you report to your boss that you did indeed beat me up as ordered and that I promised never to disturb him again—that should satisfy him."

Leon studied me, weighing his thoughts. He was a very serious young man. Finally, he gave a small nod. "Very well. I believe your advice has merit. However, I must emphasize that if you ever give Mr. Sylvia reason to doubt this agreement, I will be obliged to return and fulfill my original intention with you. Is that clear?"

"Very."

Leon nodded, got into the Caddy, and backed around so he could drive out. I had to know, so I put up a hand and walked around to the driver's door. Leon leaned out of the window.

"Leon," I said, "do you intend to specialize?"

"I do."

"In what?"

"Pediatrics."

When Leon was gone, I went inside and finished my beer. I was sweating, and not just because it was a warm day. I took a shower and changed shirts and then drove downtown and went into Doc Meyer's office.

Doc Meyer was the old-time sort of family practitioner who still saw people without appointments. He had delivered hundreds of Vineyard children and a lot of their parents as well. He was a carver of model boats, a fiddle player, and county coroner, too. He didn't like the last job because he was squeamish. Rumor had it that he'd planned to be a surgeon but just couldn't stand the cutting the job required, so he'd become a family practitioner instead. He'd been coroner for decades, out of a sense of duty to the island.

Three patients were ahead of me. I waited. Three more came into the waiting room and sat down after giving the nurse, Doc's wife, their names. When my turn came, I went in, admired his latest ship model, and asked him about the ring. There wasn't any ring, said Doc. I thanked him and left.

I caught up with the chief in, of all places, his office. He was happy to hear that I wasn't going to nose around in police business today, and he told me how to find Jim Norris's landlord up in Chilmark. He said the Chilmark police or maybe the sheriff's department had probably sent Jim's belongings back to Oregon. I drove up to Chilmark.

Chilmark is the next-to-last township up island. It's a beautiful, hilly place famous for offering the principal nude beach on the island. If you live in Chilmark, you can go to that beach if you want to, but if you don't live in Chilmark, you might be asked to leave. A lot of summer people refuse to rent anywhere but Chilmark just so they can go to that beach. Everybody to his own style, I say.

Jim Norris's landlord was not the nude-beach type. He had a fishing boat that he ran out of Menemsha and made a lot of summer money renting houses to those people who wanted to go to the nude beach and were willing to pay high prices to do so. He got by quite nicely, thank you.

Jim's cottage was tiny and sparsely furnished, but he'd taken it in the fall of the year he'd arrived and had proved so handy at fixing it up that his landlord had just let him stay there instead of throwing him out the following summer for the sake of a higher seasonal rental. On Martha's Vineyard, a lot of year-round residents rent houses in the wintertime when they're cheap, give them up for the summer trade when they're expensive, and go back to them again in the fall. Jim had been lucky. His landlord had liked him. Everybody had liked Jim. Even me.

"Look around," said his landlord when I told him of Nancy Norris's phone call. "I got some people coming in later in the week. Good thing you got here today. Lock up when you're through and stick the key over the door." He went away.

There wasn't much. Empty closet. Empty bureau, empty medicine cabinet in the bathroom. Nothing under the bed, nothing under the mattress, nothing in or under the couch, nothing down in the old overstuffed chair in the corner. Nothing in or under the bunks in the spare room or in the bureau there, nothing in the corners of the rooms. Nothing.

Finally I found the ring in an old, cracked coffee cup on the top shelf of a kitchen cabinet. Nobody but me had had a reason to look for it, and only someone looking for it would have looked in the coffee cup.

It was just what Nancy Norris had said it was—a golden metal ring with a red stone in it. Real gold? A real gemstone? No matter. Around the stone were the words LONGVIEW HIGH SCHOOL and the date 1951. Jim's mother's ring.

But it wasn't Jim's mother's ring. It was a man's ring, too big for a woman unless she had huge hands. It looked like my high school class ring, like every guy's high school class ring. Mine had my initials engraved inside. I looked inside this one. There were the initials: GHM.

I went out and locked the door. I hadn't found Jim's journal, but I did have the ring. I put the key above the door and drove home.

GHM. Jim's middle name was Singleton, according to his sister. His middle name was his mother's name. You couldn't bend Singleton enough to make it start with *M* no matter how hard you tried. Ergo, Jim's mother either really was named Singleton and for some reason had GHM's ring—probably because GHM was the child's father—or she wasn't named Singleton at all. Maybe. GHM? General H. Motors? Did Geoffrey of Monmouth have a middle initial?

As I drove through West Tisbury I wondered if Zee was home yet. I didn't think so. I wondered if I was seeing her too much too soon. She made me feel healthy, but I wasn't sure I made her feel that way. I loved her laugh. I passed the field of dancing statues and the general store, turned right, and drove toward home. I tried to remember if I'd ever seen Jim wearing the ring. I couldn't, but I couldn't remember whether he hadn't, either. Who would remember? Susie Martin would.

So instead of going straight home, I drove to the Martin place. Susie and her mother were out watering flowers. They were of the buy-them-grown-in-the-pot-so-you-can-grow-them-right-away school of flower growers. I was a plant-the-seeds-yourself man. My flowers were just beginning to push out of the earth and theirs were big and beautiful.

I asked them both if they'd ever seen Jim wearing a class ring. They hadn't. I fingered the ring in my pocket and felt perverse about not showing it to them. There was no reason not to, but I didn't. I wondered if Bilbo Baggins felt the same way when he was playing the riddle game with Gollum.

"Why do you think he had a ring?" asked Susie.

"Because his sister told me he always wore one."

"When did you talk to his sister?"

"I liked Jim," I said. "So I phoned my sympathies to his folks and his sister asked me about the ring. Apparently it never got sent back with the rest of his stuff. I didn't remember ever seeing it, but I thought maybe one of you might have."

"I never saw one," said Susie. "I would have if he'd worn one."

"It's easy to lose something like that," said her mother. "Goodness knows I've lost enough things right here at home. Years later I'll find some old earring down behind the cushions in the living room couch."

"Maybe that's what happened," I said. "Where's Billy?"

Mrs. Martin waved a hand indicating various directions. "Oh, he's off somewhere. He's not the type to stay home with the womenfolk."

I drove to the Edgartown Library, which sits prettily on North Water Street, thought by some to be the town's most ritzy locale. I asked the librarian if there was such a thing as a book that listed all of the high schools in America.

Librarians are wonderfully valuable people. This one found a book of government publications, frowned over it while she leafed through it, and then placed a polished nail upon just what I wanted: the *Educational Directory: Public School Systems*. It was put out by the National Center for Educational Statistics, whatever that might be, and was printed by—who else?—the U.S. Government Printing

Office. My tax dollars perform obscure functions at times.

"We might even have an out-of-date copy," said the librarian.

I didn't need a new edition. I sat down at a table and soon she brought me the little book and placed it in front of me. She smiled. She was happy. I smiled back. Librarians are all right.

The book listed every school system in the country in alphabetical order by state. If there had been a Longview school system somewhere in 1951, it was probably still there. School systems don't tend to disappear. Longview sounded western to me. Nobody in Massachusetts, for instance, would name their town Longview.

Smart me. There were three Longview school systems in the United States, one in Texas, one in California, and one in Washington. All three included high schools. I took some notes, thanked the librarian, and went home. I was beginning to despair over my phone bill, but nevertheless dialed directory assistance for each state and got the telephone numbers of the three schools.

Texas was two hours west of me and California and Washington were three. Most public schools were still in session, although the seniors might have been let loose by now. I dialed the Texas school. A secretary with a sweet, twangy voice answered. I gave her my name and told her where I was. People in small towns like getting calls from faraway places. She was happy.

"I have a mystery you might be able to solve," I said.

"A mystery!" People like mysteries. "How exciting! How can I help you?"

I told her about the ring and the initials. "I'd like to find out who it belonged to so I can try to return it to its owner. Do you have a 1951 yearbook?"

"Yes! We have them all right down the hall in our library. I know what you want—you want me to find out if one of our graduates had a name to match those initials!"

"Exactly. Can you do it?"

"You just hold on. This will only take a minute. It's right down the hall. This is exciting!"

It took more than a minute, but only because no one with the right initials had graduated in 1951. My helper was disappointed but undaunted. "I'm sure you'll find your man in Washington or California!"

I thanked her and called Longview, California. Ten minutes later I had the name.

George Harrison Martin. George. My fishing buddy, George.

I didn't bother calling Washington.

* 14 *

Jim Norris's mother had George Martin's high school class ring when she died. Jim Norris always wore the ring, but he'd never worn it on Martha's Vineyard. Instead, he'd hidden it away in a coffee cup. I looked at my watch. The library was still open. I went back. The librarian was still on duty. I asked her if she kept old copies of *Time* magazine.

"I want to look at that story about George Martin. Remember it? Year before last, I think."

She nodded. "Of course I remember it. George has become a loyal supporter of the library. I know we still have that magazine, but I'll have to get it for you. We only have room enough for the more recent editions of our magazines here on the main floor and that story came out two years ago this month."

She went out and came back with the magazine. I sat down and read the story again.

It was a good-natured human interest story amid a long piece on the life-styles of America's economic whiz kids. George had been one of them. Forced by a mid-forties heart attack to reconsider his priorities, he had done the seemingly impossible: he had sold out completely and returned to the simple life on Martha's Vineyard, where he was completely happy. There was a picture of him down on the beach looking right at home with the local surf casters. There was also a brief résumé of his life.

He had been born into a working-class family in Longview, California. His parents ran a mom-and-pop grocery store. He'd been drafted and had served in the Korean war, where he'd been captured and imprisoned for several months before escaping. After getting home to the States, he'd attended Brown on the G.I. Bill and academic scholarships and, upon graduation, had immediately seen the promise of high technology and started his own company. He married Marge White, whom he'd met at a cocktail party, and they had two children, William and Susan.

He was a millionaire by the time he was thirty-five and a multimillionaire by the time he was forty. He liked fishing and hunting, but had little time for either. After a routine physical he was advised by his doctor to slow down, but he hadn't and one day had a mild heart attack. He tried then to slow down, but didn't. Second and third heart attacks persuaded him to change his life-style completely. His associates didn't think he could do it, but he did. He no longer saw much of his old friends, but had become an islander. He was happy and had no regrets. He was content with his Jeep, shotguns, and fishing gear.

I reread the part about Korea. He'd been captured on his very first patrol and had been reported missing in action and later presumed dead. His parents had been shocked when he'd shown up almost a year later. There was no mention of a high school sweetheart.

I got the ring out of my pocket and rolled it between thumb and fingers, thinking.

Jim Norris had showed up on the Vineyard a couple of months after the *Time* article appeared. He'd gotten a job easily because there was a lot of construction on the island and good carpenters were always in demand. He'd taken a place up island and had soon joined the fishing crowd at Wasque, where he and George met and hit it off. Why had he come to Wasque when there was good fishing up island a lot closer to his house? Why hadn't he joined the fishermen at Squibnocket or Gay Head or Lobsterville? Why had he taken to coming all the way down to Chappaquiddick for his bluefishing?

He had the ring and he'd found out who it belonged to, maybe the same way I'd found out, maybe because his wanderings had taken him to Longview, California. He'd thought what I was thinking—that George Harrison Martin was his father. Then, later, he'd seen the *Time* article and come to the Vineyard to see his old man.

But when he got here, he'd taken off the ring. Why? Because he didn't want George to see it. Why?

The librarian came over. "I'm sorry, J.W., but it's closing time. You can come back tomorrow."

I thanked her and went home. There was still a lot of light. The fish were in, but I decided to let them live another day. I sat down and read the latest *Gazette*, looking for the latest rumors about drugs and cops. I had to look hard because the *Gazette* prefers to dwell upon the beauties of the Vineyard and the dangers of overdevelopment. I found the story four pages in. A two-inch report of a number of officials declining comment.

I had a beer and made a refrigerator omelet out of eggs and the odds and ends left over from earlier meals. I thought Zee would have liked my omelet, but she wasn't there, so I ate her share. When I had everything washed up, I drove up to the hospital to see George.

He was now in a private room and looked good.

"I don't know why I'm here," he grumped. "I'm ready to break out."

"Watch television."

"Have you watched television lately?"

"I watched the late news a couple of nights back."

"It's summer rerun time. Television is bad enough in the winter. It's worse in the summer."

"You should probably watch soap operas. They're the same all year round, I think."

"What I want to see is a bluefish taking my plug."

"Read a book."

He grinned. "Fuck you, J.W."

"I just came across that *Time* story," I said. "I came up here so I could hobnob with a member of the upper classes."

"It's too bad you never learned to read," said George. "If you could, you'd know I'm about as upper class as you are, which obviously isn't very. My people are barely off the boat."

"Don't get snooty about it." I sat down. "Martin sounds like an English name. Your people from there originally?"

"That's a strange question coming from you. In all the years I've known you, I don't think I ever heard you ask anyone a single thing about their past."

"His past," I said, "or her past. 'Their' is a plural pronoun, not a singular one."

"What?"

"I'm a strange sort of guy," I said. "Humor me."

"You humor me first. Why don't you ask people the

usual sort of questions—Where do you come from? What do you do for a living?—that sort of thing. It's normal, but you don't do it."

"I used to ask a lot of questions for a living. Maybe I'm just out of the habit. I remember once I was at a party and suddenly got the idea that, since most of us there didn't know one another, we should all agree to talk about anything but what we did for a living. I thought it would be fun and that maybe it would have some effect on how we treated each other. You know, we wouldn't treat each other in terms of our jobs. We wouldn't talk one way to someone because we knew she was a doctor or because she dug ditches. I think maybe it had to do with the fact that I was a cop and as soon as people learned that they started acting differently."

"How did it go?"

"It didn't go. A guy who was talking to me when I suggested it became quite upset. He insisted on knowing what I did for a living. I thought he was joking, but he wasn't. After a few minutes he got red in the face and blurted out, 'Well, I'm a minister!' And he walked away and never spoke to me again. Later somebody told me he was a pastoral counselor."

George nodded. "That's what I like about Wasque. Down there nobody cares what you do. They only worry about having you cross their lines. But now here you are, asking me about my ancestors."

"That was just a feint. I do have some questions I'd like to ask you, though. I think they're important, but I'd prefer not to tell you why right now because I'm not sure yet just where all this will lead."

He looked understandably perplexed.

"I do think they're important," I repeated. "I'll even tell you why I want to know, if you insist. But I'd rather you didn't."

He grunted and looked at me hard. "Well, I owe you my life, I think, so how can I refuse?"

"You can refuse. I won't even promise to tell you anything later. I haven't worked that out yet."

"All right. Ask away. I don't think I have any skeletons in my closet."

Everyone had skeletons somewhere, I thought. Something they'd just as soon no one ever found out about. But I needed to know about the ring.

"Straight to it, then. Tell me about your girlfriends when you were, say, in high school. For example, did you have a steady girl?"

A quizzical little smile appeared on his face. Then he shook his head. "Jesus, that goes a long ways back. No, no steady girl. A lot of the guys had steady girls, of course, but I was working at the store and trying for a scholarship, so I was too busy to interest any of the girls too much. I dated, of course. The movies now and then. A couple of proms. But I wasn't into school sports or the sort of things that girls liked to do. Why do you . . . ? Oops, forgot, you don't want to tell me why you're interested."

"Not yet, at least. What happened after you graduated? I know you got drafted, but when? Right away, or was there a delay?"

"No delay. I'd gotten a scholarship to Brown. I wanted to go east to school. I'd never been east of the Sierra Nevadas. But then Uncle Sam sent his invitation. I suppose I could have tried to get a student deferment, but I didn't. I figured that after my two years I'd have the G.I. Bill and the scholarship to help me through college." He gave a wry look. "Of course it never occurred to me that I'd actually have to go overseas, so when I got my shipping orders it was quite a shock."

I'd gotten the same shock a war later.

"When did you ship out?"

"I'll never forget. January fifth, 1952. A date imbedded in my memory. For most of the next year I thought my last view of the States was going to have been the San Diego airport."

"You were captured soon after you got over there."

He nodded. "My first combat patrol. To this day I think somebody just screwed up. The whole patrol was green except for the sergeant. We didn't know what we were doing. It was dark, then the sergeant got hit and then we got separated and then I got lost and I blundered right into a gook patrol. They knew what they were doing, I didn't. I never fired a shot. It was that quick. I'm still not sure why they didn't just kill me."

"They kept you for several months?"

"Yes. They grilled me for a long time. When I got back I learned that some people called it brainwashing. But I was so green that I didn't have anything in my brain, so there wasn't anything to wash. Hell, I didn't even know the men in my own patrol, so after a while they pretty much gave up on me. I read a lot of communist tracts and lost a lot of weight, but the time came when I was a more experienced prisoner than my guards were experienced guards, so I got away. It was a long walk. I lived on roots and grubs, but by that time I could eat anything. I almost got shot by my own people, but they missed the first time and I yelled before they tried again, and that was that. A year in the battle zone and I never fired a shot in anger, never really even saw combat. Odd. They kept me in a hospital for a while to fatten me up, then they sent me home with some medals. George Martin, hero. I rode in a parade down Main Street in Longview."

"Then what?"

"I contacted Brown and told them my story and they said to come on, so I did. I spent the next four years there, got out, and went to work."

"Any girls while you were in college?"

"You're stuck on girls, J.W. Sure, there were girls. I was a little older, a little wiser, maybe. I liked some girls and some of them liked me. But nothing serious or long term. Hell, I can't even remember their names." He frowned. "Let's see, there was Bess and there was Elaine. Elaine was studying archaeology or something like that at Radcliffe. Bright girl. Then there was . . . what was her name? A lot of fun. Liked western movies. A John Wayne fan . . ."

"But nobody serious?"

"No. I was studying hard and I had a job on the side. I didn't have time to be a real undergraduate. I felt old and I was in a hurry. No, I never got serious until later, when I met Marge. Then I was serious enough to want to marry her and I did. Twenty-two years now. Smartest thing I ever did."

"When you were a prisoner, were you allowed to keep your personal belongings? Your watch, your comb, that sort of thing?"

"You jest, my boy. They stripped us down to the skin and took everything we owned. They gave us rags to wear. They even took our dogtags. Everything. Later, sometimes, we got other gear. Soap now and then. Some disinfectant. Nothing sharp."

So he hadn't taken his ring to Korea, otherwise it would still be there. He'd parted with it before that.

"Let's go back to the time before you were shipped out. Tell me about that."

He raised an eyebrow. "You mean, did I have any girlfriends?"

"Did you?"

His smile got a little stiff. "Sure. What soldier doesn't? We all found them when they let us off base for a few hours."

"I know," I said. "I remember what boot camp was like. Looking back, it doesn't seem as bad as it seemed then. I remember some girls. But none of them were serious." I put a smile on my face. "But a few of the guys got engaged. A couple even got married. Did anything like that happen to anyone you knew?"

He looked at me and the little smile slid off his face.

"Think back," I said. "Did any of the guys get engaged? Buy a ring for the new girl? Give her the old school ring to cement the engagement till he could buy her the real thing?"

George stared at me.

"Maybe it was later," I said. "Maybe between the end of training and the time you were shipped out. You knew you were not going to stay stateside and weren't going to Germany, but to Korea. I remember how I felt when I learned where I was going. . . ."

He held up his hand and I stopped. "You know, don't you?"

"Tell me about the girl," I said.

He looked at the ceiling. "God." He was silent for a while, then: "There really was a girl. Afterward I almost thought sometimes that there hadn't been. I know there was, but later she seemed like part of a dream." He looked at me, then past me into space, then at me again. "I met her three days before I was to be shipped out. I was in San Diego just waiting and drinking and trying to live a lot before I went off to God knows what. We hit it off right away. I can't explain it. We talked and talked and it was like nothing that had ever happened to me before. She was pretty, I remember that. But that wasn't what made me like her. She'd walked on the wild side some. She told me a little about it. She was nice, but she ran with a tough crowd. She wanted out." He rubbed his chin. "We went down to Mexico and we got married. We had two nights together and then I got shipped out. Marlina Singleton. Marlina . . ."

"You bought her a wedding ring?"

"No. We were in a hurry. I gave her my class ring. We used that at the wedding. The guy who married us didn't bat an eye. He'd had a lot of business from San Diego."

"What happened to Marlina?"

"It's been years since I thought about all this. Jesus, it seems so long ago. I don't know what happened to her. I got a letter from her in Korea just before I went on that first patrol. One letter. Something had happened. Some kind of trouble. She had to leave town, but she said she'd write as soon as she could. I wrote back, but a week later I was captured and I never heard from her again. While I was a prisoner I'd been reported missing, presumed dead. Maybe she heard that story. Maybe not. When I got back to the States I tried to trace her. I looked for her for a month, all through August, but it was as though she'd dropped off the earth. So in the fall I went east to school. I looked for her some more the next summer, but I never found her."

"If she was in trouble and had to get out of town, maybe

she didn't want to be found. The army knew you were married, didn't it?"

"Yes. I made her beneficiary of my life insurance."

"She may have thought they'd be able to trace her if she used her married name. Maybe she was afraid that if the army could find her, someone else might be able to, too. She was just a young girl who maybe didn't want to be found by anybody."

"I thought of that," he said. "I didn't know her friends or her family. I didn't even know where she came from. Utah, I think. Some little town in the desert. I don't think she ever told me its name. I talked to the army and the police and I went back to the bar where we'd met. But two years had passed. Nobody knew anything." He looked at me. "Are you going to tell me what this is all about?"

"I don't know much," I said. "I do know one thing that you should probably know, too. Marlina is dead. She died probably thinking she was a widow."

"How did it happen?"

"Natural causes," I said. "It was a long time ago. There was nothing you could have done."

* 15 *

I made another telephone call to Oregon and to Nancy Norris. I told her I'd found the ring. She was happy.

"Mom will be pleased. It means a lot to her. Did you find the journal?"

"No. Ask your mom if Jim's mother's first name was Marlina."

"Of course. Just a moment." Then she was back, surprised. "Why, yes. How did you know?"

"The ring belonged to her husband. I traced it. I found him."

"Jim's father?"

"Her husband, at least. When was Jim's birthday?"

"October fourth."

"What year?"

"1952."

"The husband was probably the father, then. The man doesn't know and I haven't decided yet whether to tell him. All he knows is that Marlina died a long time ago. He doesn't know about the child."

"I'd like to know his name. I'm sure Mom would, too."

"I'm not sure I'll tell you. Can I keep the ring for a few days?"

"Oh, dear, I don't know what to think. This is so . . ."

"Don't decide everything right now. Tell your folks that Jim's father is a very fine man who has a family he loves. We'll talk again in a few days. Right now, things are a bit unsettled here, and I'd like to keep the ring awhile. It may be useful in clearing things up. Is that okay?"

"All right," she said. "You will call?"

"Yes. In a few days."

I had a beer. The summer night was warm, so I went out and sat on the screen porch. Across the Sound I could see the lights of Cape Cod twinkling in the clear air. The wind moved through the trees. Above, the Milky Way stretched across the sky. The moon hung in the branches of a tree, thin and pale. I got another beer and put on a Ricky Skaggs tape and went out onto the porch again. Ricky sang songs about loving and losing. It was a lonesome kind of night. I thought of Zee. When the tape was over, I finished the beer and went to bed, still unable to erase thoughts of Zee, even if I'd tried, which I didn't.

I was having breakfast—smoked bluefish, red onion, and cream cheese on a toasted bagel, washed down with coffee—on the porch with the sun coming up over the Sound. The way God intended man to live. The phone rang. It was Jim Norris's landlord, mad as a wet hen.

"What the hell you go busting things up like that, Jackson? You had the God-damned key! Why'd you bust the door down? Tell me that, you . . . I'm gonna sue you, you no-account—"

So much for my morning in Eden. "What are you talking about?"

"You know what I'm talking about. You're the only one who's been up to Jim's cabin. You had the key! Why'd you kick the door in? Why'd you throw things around? Why'd you tear things up? I'm going to sue you for every cent you cost me, you—"

"I didn't kick the door down. I left everything just the way I found it. The key's right over the door, where you told me to leave it. When did this trouble happen?"

It occurred to him that maybe I hadn't done it, but he was still hot. "You know danged well when it happened! It happened when you was there!"

"No. Everything was fine when I left. I'd be a fool to kick the door down when I had the key, don't you think?"

"Well, by God! Well . . . well, you was the only one up there, wasn't you?"

"I guess not. Somebody else was there later. Somebody who didn't know where the key was."

"Well, I suppose it could have been. I mean, you knew where the key was. . . ."

"You gave it to me. You say things were torn up inside?"

"Jesus, you should see it! Furniture cut up, things tossed every which way! A real mess! And me with people coming in later this week! I tell you, when I get the guy who . . ."

He almost but not quite apologized before he rang off. I went out and finished breakfast, then weeded in the garden for an hour. I don't like to weed for more than an hour because I get bored. I get bored in museums, too, after a couple of hours. Maybe I have a short attention span. Not for Zee, of course. I thought I could stand her for quite a long stretch at a time.

I wanted some quahogs, so I got my rake and basket and went down to Anthier's Pond (Sengekontacket Pond to those of you who speak Wompanoag). I parked at the Rod and Gun Club and waded out to the point beyond the clubhouse. I've had good luck there, as a rule, but lately the quahogs are getting thinned out. It took me an hour to get a mess, but I had a little of everything—some little-necks, cherrystones, and growlers for chowder. I waded back, went home, rinsed off the quahogs and put them in the fridge after popping a half-dozen littlenecks as a special treat for me. Littlenecks on the half shell are hard to beat, being surpassed only by oysters on the half shell. But since oysters are often soft and squishy in the sum-mertime, littlenecks are the champions of that season. Thinking of this, I opened a dozen more and wolfed them down. Thank you, God.

At noon I drove up to Oak Bluffs and went into the Fireside. After a while, Bonzo came in, gave me a big smile, and came over to the bar. I bought him a beer.

"Gee, thanks," said Bonzo. "Say. J.W., when we going to go fishing again?"

"Soon," I said. "Bonzo, were you working here Saturday before last?"

"Sure," said Bonzo. "I'm here every Saturday. I got work to do here. I got to do the sweeping, you know. People spill drinks and drop things all the time. Pretzels and like that, and they break glasses sometimes. I gotta be here for that, especially Saturdays." He drank his beer.

"Do you know Tim Mello?"

"Sure, J.W., I know almost everybody, and they all know me. I got a lot of friends in here. I got friends all over the island, I'll bet."

"I'll bet you do. Do you remember Tim Mello talking about taking the *Bluefin* down to Wasque rip? Did you hear him talking about that on that Saturday night?"

Bonzo looked aghast that I should ask such a dumb question. "Jeez, J.W., sure I heard him. Everybody heard him." Bonzo laughed. "Everybody thought it was pretty funny, him having to take the *Bluefin* down to the rips with two little old people from New Bedford!"

I grinned at Bonzo. "Do you remember when Tim was supposed to go fishing with those two old people?"

"Sure I do, J.W. He was gonna be there at eight o'clock Monday morning. To catch the tide, you know, just like when you and me go fishing. We always catch the tide. You know that. You're a funny guy, J.W. Sometimes you seem to forget things, you know?"

"Do you remember Billy Martin and Jim Norris being in here when Tim was talking about his job at Wasque?"

Bonzo frowned. "Gee, J.W., there was a lot of people here, you know. It was a Saturday night, and we do a lot of business on Saturday night." Suddenly his face brightened around his empty eyes. "Oh, yeah! Sure, they were here. I remember now. You know why? Because I thought they were going to have a fight, but they didn't. Lemme see . . . first Jim comes in and he's looking kind of low, like. And he has a beer and I say, 'Hi, Jim,' and then in comes Billy later and he's mad. I can see that. I didn't say, 'Hi, Billy,' because when Billy's mad . . . well, he's got a temper, you know? But I watched him and he went right over to Jim and I thought they might be gonna have a fight. But they didn't. Jim started talking to him, and after a while Billy wasn't mad anymore and just looked funny instead, and they sat there and that was when Tim came in and told about his new job for the *Bluefin* and we all laughed." Bonzo paused and sipped his beer and then said, "You know, J.W., it's a lot nicer to laugh than to fight. It's a lot more fun."

"You're right about that," I said. I bought us each another beer. Around us the noisy voices of the noontime drinkers lifted and rattled through the rafters. At a booth

I saw a quick exchange of money and something uniden-
tifiable in a white packet. The smell of marijuana mixed
with that of tobacco and beer.

"Hey, Bonzo," I said. "Can I borrow your tape recorder?"

He was flattered, I think. "Gee, J.W., sure you can. You
know what's mine is yours. You know that. You're my
friend. Hey, you gonna get some bird sounds, too? Can I
hear 'em when you get 'em, J.W.? Can I?"

"Sure. Thanks, Bonzo."

I picked up the tape recorder and mike at his mother's
house. It was a nice rig. Expensive and powerful. Bonzo
didn't have many expenses, so he'd splurged on a good
piece of equipment. I bought a pack of tapes and put
everything in the Landcruiser.

I felt like I'd been away from Zee for a long time. I
hadn't seen her, in fact, for almost forty hours. I'd known
her eight days. I felt in love. It was scary, bubbly, despair-
ing, hopeful, brainless. I drove to the hospital and went to
the emergency ward. I saw Zee, but she didn't see me. She
was laughing with a young doctor. Joy was possible for her
without me. They were a good-looking couple. I was
jealous. I went away and visited George. He was about to
go home.

"Bonanza!" he said. "They're letting me out. You leave
any fish in the sea?"

"I think there's one left. Maybe two."

"God, I hate hospitals. They're unhealthy places. People
die in them all the time. Almost nobody ever dies fishing."

That was my line about hospitals being unhealthy, but I
let it pass. "Perfect logic, George. How are you getting
home?"

"Billy's coming to get me. One o'clock sharp. I told him

I didn't want to be in here one minute longer than necessary!"

I looked at my watch. A quarter to one. "Okay," I said, "I'll get out of your way. See you on the beach, buddy."

I went out and stood inside the doors leading to the parking lot. When Billy drove in and parked the Wagoneer, I walked out and met him as if by accident.

"Hey, Billy," I said, "I've been looking for you."

"What for?"

"You ever see Jim Norris wear a class ring?"

"A class ring?"

"Yeah. I talked to Jim's sister out in Oregon and she said that he always wore a class ring. But I never saw him wearing one and neither did your sister. Did you?"

"No. Why?"

"Because I found it. I've got it at home."

"What! I thought . . . Mom said that you . . ." He paused thoughtfully. "No. Come to think of it, she never said you didn't have it. But she didn't think you had it."

"I missed it the first time I looked, but I found it later. It's at home now. I'm going to send it back to Jim's folks tomorrow. You never saw him wear it, eh?"

"No." He glanced at his watch.

"Yeah, you're supposed to pick up your old man," I said. "I just saw him. Tell him that I'm going down to Wasque this afternoon to catch the last fish before he can get there."

Billy grinned. "Okay, J.W., I'll tell him."

"I gotta go," I said, "or I'll miss the tide."

"You fishermen are all alike." Billy smiled, shaking his head. Billy was not a fisherman.

I went home and got things ready for the afternoon. It took about an hour, and I had a couple of beers while I

worked. When everything was ready, I drove to Katama.
Traffic wasn't bad because it was early afternoon. People
who planned to go to the beach were already there, and it
was too early for them to be going home. The sun was hot
and bright and high in the sky. There was a thin line of
clouds far to the south.

When I got to Katama, I drove onto the beach and
parked behind a dune. I got a beer out of the cooler.
When I finished the beer, I drove back home. I parked the
Landcruiser across the end of my driveway, locked the
doors, and walked down to my house. When I neared the
house I could see a yellow sportscar. Billy drove such a car,
as I recalled.

* 16 *

I circled through the trees until I came up behind my storage shed. I peeked inside and saw that no search had been made there, yet. I saw no one in the rear windows of my house, so I slipped quickly up to the outdoor shower. Under the house, behind the shower, was Bonzo's tape recorder. The mike was hanging from a rafter in the living room. Bonzo's good equipment might even pick up sounds from adjoining rooms as well. I popped out the tape in the machine and put in a new one, then peeked in through my bedroom window. There was Billy at my desk, looking in drawers and cubbyholes. I had a good view of his back and his busy hands. He was trying to be thorough yet leave things looking undisturbed. A hard task for a professional, and Billy was no professional. He was an amateur. He slammed a drawer shut and cursed.

I went around to the front of the house and eased up onto the porch. I peeked in a living room window. No Billy. I went inside, glad that I'd oiled the hinges earlier that afternoon. I went to my bedroom and stuck my head into the doorway.

"Hi, Billy," I said.

He was at my bedside table, his back to the door. He

jumped and spun around, his eyes wild for a moment. But then they narrowed.

"Jesus, J.W., you scared the hell out of me! I didn't hear you drive in."

"You find anything, Billy?"

"Find anything? No. I wasn't looking for anything." He put a grin on his face. "I found out what you read in bed." He half turned around and picked up my bedtime book. I have a book by my bed, a book by the toilet for throne reading (poetry, usually, stories and essays being too long for that locale,) a living room book by the couch, and a glove-compartment book in the Landcruiser. "The Bible," said Billy, waving the book at me before putting it back. "I never took you for a Bible reader, J.W."

"It's a good book," I said. "Mindless sex and violence, religious fanatics, war and pestilence, sin and salvation. They should make a movie out of it or a TV series. I'm having a beer. You want one?" I wanted him in the living room.

"Sure," said Billy. What else could he say? He followed me into the living room and waited while I got two Molsons from the fridge. I gestured toward a chair and we both sat down. Billy was working out his story. I brought the ring out of my pocket.

"Here it is," I said. "Jim's ring."

His eyes fixed on it.

"It's got initials inside," I said. "GHM. George Harrison Martin. Your dad's name, your dad's ring. Jim's ring. Sit back, Billy, and relax. I'm going to tell you a story."

I told him about George and Marlina, how they found and lost each other and how Marlina ended up in Oregon pregnant and ill. I told him how a young nurse, Mrs.

Norris, who wanted children but couldn't have them, adopted Marlina's child and got the ring, and how, later, she gave it to the boy.

"Then Jim took to the road," I said. "He liked to work for a while and then move on. Maybe one day he came to a town called Longview. Maybe that's how it happened. Or maybe he traced his father just like I did. No matter. He found his father's name.

"But it didn't do him any good because he had no way of knowing where his old man was. Then two years ago, in June 1985, he read that story in *Time* and knew where he was. Jim came up that summer to meet him in person. He knew from the article that George liked to fish, so he managed to meet him on the beach. But he didn't want his dad to know who he was, so he put the ring away and didn't wear it for fear that George might recognize it.

"Jim was a genuinely nice guy. Everybody who knew him says so. He knew George had a new family and he didn't want to be a long-lost son suddenly appearing on the scene. All he wanted was to get to know his old man. And he did that. Better yet, he and George got close. They liked one another. And Jim liked Susie, too. And I even think he tried to like you.

"But then something he hadn't expected happened—Susie fell in love with him. He knew that she was his half sister, but she didn't know he was her half brother. Since he didn't want her to know who he really was, he decided to bag it and head back to Oregon. He'd found out that his dad was a terrific guy and that was enough. He didn't need to rake the past up and make things more complicated for the Martins, so he just decided to leave.

"But you love your sister. She's probably the only person you do love, but you do love her. And when you found her crying because Jim had given her the cold shoulder, you blew your stack and went after him. Big brother coming to little sister's rescue. Very commendable.

"When you found Jim up at the Fireside, you were ready to punch him out, but he managed to get you to listen to him and he told you the truth about himself—that he was George's son and that your sister was his sister and that the two of you were brothers and that he was going back out west and wouldn't be back. He told you about the ring and about the story in *Time*.

"And that might have been the end of it, but it wasn't. You knew that Jim could change his mind and show up again, and that if he ever told the truth about himself and backed it up with the ring, he stood a good chance of inheriting a large hunk of George's money. Bad news for you, because you spend money so fast that you have to sell dope to maintain your life-style."

I finished my beer.

"You can't prove any of this," said Billy.

"Just as you and Jim were talking, you heard Tim Mello making jokes about his charter to take the *Bluefin* to fish the Wasque rip at eight o'clock Monday morning and you get an idea. The *Nellie Grey* has had some gasline problems, and maybe people will think they never really got fixed. You buddy up to Jim, brother to brother like, and you tell him the two of you should take one last fishing trip together before he leaves. You tell him you'll make Wasque at eight A.M. You need to have a boat nearby to rescue you when the *Nellie Grey* blows up, and now you know the *Bluefin* will be there.

"And it works like a charm. You go out from Edgartown and you can see the *Bluefin* coming down from Vineyard Haven. You wave at us there at the Cape Pogue light, then cosh Jim, loosen a fitting on a gasline and go up on the foredeck so you'll be away from the explosion. I expect you sloshed some gas around in the cabin first and had some kind of timer made out of a clock and a battery or something like that, so when its spark detonated the fumes you were almost overboard already. Then you made your heroic effort to save your buddy/brother Jim, but all in vain. The *Bluefin* pulls you out of the drink and, lo, you're almost a hero, not a murderer at all."

"You're crazy," said Billy. "You're full of shit. You can't prove a thing."

I held up the ring. "I've got motive and opportunity. Your sister and the guys at the boatyard will swear that the *Nellie Grey* had no gasoline leaks. Ergo, the explosion was no accident. Once the cops have reason to believe that, they'll do a lot better job of examining the evidence still out there where the *Nellie Grey* went down, and I imagine they'll find some stuff they overlooked before. Battery and wires, maybe. Maybe whatever it was you coshed Jim with. I think the D.A. will be able to stick this one to you pretty good."

"I'm getting out of here." He stood up. I stood up. He sat down. I sat down.

"You knew about the ring from the time Jim talked to you that Saturday night at the Fireside, when I imagine he told you about it. You knew that you had to get rid of it because it was the one tangible object that could tie Jim to your father. But you couldn't steal it the next day because Jim was home most of the day packing his gear. And you couldn't get it later because you were in the hospital while the authorities packed up his stuff and sent it west. You thought the ring had been shipped west with the rest of his things, and that wasn't too bad because nobody out there had any reason to link Jim and your father together.

"But then I got the call from Jim's sister about the ring being missing, and I told your mother and sister about it and that night somebody broke into Jim's house and tore things up looking for something. As you might guess, I figure that somebody was you, because your mother and sister told you what I'd told them—that the ring hadn't gotten to Oregon.

"But you didn't find the ring because I already had it and knew what it was. But just to be sure, I set up this latest little housebreaking effort of yours. I told you that the ring was here and that I'd be gone. If it meant nothing to you, you'd have stayed away. But here you are. I watched you for a while through the window while you went through my desk. You're not a nice guy, Billy. All your family's rotten genes must have settled in you."

"I'll deny everything. My dad can afford the best lawyers in the United States."

"Sure, Billy. Whether he will hire them is another question. After all, you killed his son, your brother, in cold blood. There is one thing I'm only half sure of. Maybe you can tell me. Jim's journal is missing. It wasn't in his house when I found the ring and it never got home to Oregon with his other things. The only place I can imagine it being is out in the wreck of the *Nellie Grey*. I figure Jim told you about it and you said you'd like to have a look at it before he went west, so he brought it along on the fishing trip."

"What do I care about his journal?"

"You cared for the same reason you cared about the ring—because he might have written down the truth about how he found his father. I expect that the book probably got burned in the fire, but there should still be bits of it out there. Enough to identify it, at least."

Billy sat there. Then he leaned forward. "Jim was a fool. If he'd kept his mouth shut, he'd be back in Oregon right now. You're a fool, too. If you'd kept your mouth shut, I wouldn't have known what you're up to. Now I know everything you know, and you've got to go, too."

He pulled a revolver out from under his shirt. It looked like my old police .38. It was.

"Locks on gun cabinets don't mean much, Jackson," said Billy, with a crooked smile on his face. He pointed the gun at me. I felt sweat break out on my forehead. "Any last words?" he asked.

* 17 *

"A couple," I said, trying to sound unruffled. "First, there's a locked Landcruiser blocking the end of the driveway, so you'll have a hard time getting out of here. You may make it, but your car won't. It can't knock down enough trees to reach the highway. Second, since I was smart enough to set you up, don't you imagine that I'm smart enough not to make myself a sitting duck? Remember, I'm the guy who knew you were a murderer. I'm not like poor Jim, who never suspected a thing before you killed him.

"Somebody is listening to us, Billy, and recording every word. You shoot me and your goose is really cooked. You'll go up forever."

"You're lying. Say good-bye, Jackson."

"Look up at that beam. See that mike? Don't worry about me jumping you. Your bullet can get to me quicker than I can get to you."

Billy looked at me with wild eyes. Could I see insanity within them, or was that only a reflection of my fear? His smile was gone. A shadow seemed to flicker across his face. Then he glanced up, quickly down at me again, then up once more. The second time, he saw it. His eyes whipped back down again.

"We have a stalemate," I suggested. "I have the ring, you have the pistol you're pointing at me, and someone has a tape of our conversation."

"Maybe I can find your friend when I'm through with you."

I heard the word "maybe" like a sailor hears a bell buoy in the fog. "Maybe" sounded like safety. It told me where I was. I took up the word for myself. "Maybe you can, but probably not. You don't even know where those wires lead."

What immortal hand or eye framed Billy's symmetry? He stared at me, then suddenly laughed. "Hey, J.W., I got you, didn't I? You fell for this act just the way I thought you would! Here!" He reversed the pistol and tossed it at me. "How about another beer?" He laughed pretty authentically and got up and went to the fridge and brought back two Molsons. "Here, J.W. Next time, I'll buy.

"You think I didn't realize you wanted me down here for some reason? You think if I wanted that ring, I couldn't have had it? Hell, Jim said he'd give it to me if I wanted it. He showed me his journal, so why wouldn't he show me the ring? And do you think I didn't see that mike when I came in? Jesus, J.W., do you think I'm blind?

"Wise up, J.W. I didn't take the ring because Jim didn't want Dad to know who he was, and Jim and I agreed that if I took it Dad might see it sometime and start asking questions Jim didn't want to answer. You got half of the motives right, J.W., but you fucked up the other ones. Jim died in an accident and I came down here knowing that you thought you were setting me up. Jesus, J.W., you've been running around in circles for nothing. Come on, drink up. The joke's on you!"

It was pretty convincing theater. I popped the cylinder

and saw that it was loaded, then snapped it back and looked at Billy. He smiled. I smiled. I never kept the gun loaded; Billy had loaded it.

"I think it would be nice if you went down to the police station and made a statement," I said. "I don't think it was smart of you to keep all this information to yourself. It gave me some funny ideas and it may give other people funnier ones. A statement from you might clear the air a lot."

Billy smiled. "Sure. That's a good idea. I'll do that right away. Just as long as nobody tells Dad. Jim didn't want him to know. . . ." His voice trailed off as I looked at him over the sights of the pistol. I felt my finger tighten on the trigger. "Hey!" he said. "What are you doing?"

I squeezed the trigger and saw the hammer rise a bit. "Bang!" I said. I lowered the gun. "Just a joke, Billy."

"Sure." Billy laughed. "I'll pay for the damage I did to the gun cabinet, don't worry about that. You know, I saw your shadow when you were watching me through the window. I just messed things up as part of the joke, you understand." His eyes kept straying up to the mike. "Well, I better be going." He stood up. "How about the ring, J.W.? I'm thinking that maybe it's best that Dad have it after all. I mean, Jim's dead, so it can't matter to him anyhow. Besides, I'm going to give my statement to the police and it's bound to leak out anyway, don't you think?"

"I'll keep it," I said. "I'll be going downtown to make a statement of my own. I'll talk to your dad, then think about whether he should have it or whether I should send it out to the Norrises in Oregon."

"Oh." He licked his lips. "Well . . ." He drank from his beer and looked around for a place to set it down.

"Hey," I said. "I hear they're going to bust a bunch of

people down here one of these days. Sylvia, maybe. Some other people. Some people you know. I'll bet that if you were to help the good guys out, they might not nail you as hard as they can right now, what with you being a pusher in college and all. You know what I mean? It would be nice if they could get some of the bigwigs, don't you think?"

"What do you mean?" He emptied his bottle and stood up. I did the same.

"I mean it would be something in your favor if you could name some names and give some testimony to the DEA and the others who'll be making this bust. If you could tie Sylvia directly to the operation, a lot of people would think you were a terrific person."

"I don't know anything about Sylvia. I'm through with all that now."

"Oh, come on, Billy, grow up. You can name names. You can name one in particular, and you know who I mean."

"No, I don't."

"I mean Maria Sylvia, your source. She likes young guys like you, and one way she keeps them is by supplying them with some chemical adventure to supplement her maturing charms. I imagine she's supplying the tennis pro or whoever else is on her string, so you needn't think you'll be betraying your own true love if you testify. You be a good citizen and maybe the narcs can tie Sylvia to his wife's habit of dispensing chemicals to her swains. I mean, she has to get her drugs from somebody, doesn't she? You do that and maybe I won't push for the cops bringing the *Nellie Grey* up from the bottom and going over her with a fine-tooth comb."

"What makes you think that Mrs. Sylvia gave me any drugs?"

"She's got something that makes the boys love her, and you got your stuff from somebody named Sylvia. It wasn't the old man and it wasn't your ex-buddy Danny Sylvia, because he's been in California while you've been at Brown. Who else would it be but your good friend Maria Sylvia?"

"You can't prove it."

"Who's talking proof, kid? Right now I have a good case against you and I think I can convince the cops to dig deeper than you might want them to. I don't have to have proof. All I need to have is evidence. And I've got that."

Billy's brain was busy. "If I testify, you'll let this other thing drop?"

"I said I wouldn't push it."

He thought some more. "I want the ring and I want the tape."

"Afterward. After you talk to the cops about you and Jim and after you testify against Maria Sylvia and your other pals in the drug biz. After all that, you can have the ring and tape. Not before."

"Tapes can be copied. You could give me one and still have another one."

"You have a paranoid streak in you, Billy. You've got to learn to trust people."

"Sure." I could almost see thoughts and counterthoughts racing through his mind. "You're wrong about me killing Jim, you know. You're wrong about that."

"Okay, Billy, we've got that taped. Anything else you'd like to get on the record?"

"You can't prove anything. No one can, because I didn'
do anything."

"You're repeating yourself now, Billy."

"It's that Bonzo, isn't it? It's him you've got on the othe
end of that wire. Who else would it be? You could talk him
into anything."

"He loaned me some equipment. He thinks I'm recording bird calls."

Billy stared at me, comprehension appearing on hi
face. And as he comprehended, fury filled his eyes. First
hot, then cold hate reached out toward me. Then the hate
pulled back and hid, and Billy's voice was almost normal
"He's not there, then. He never was. Nobody was. You
lied. There isn't anybody listening."

"Nobody. But there is a tape. And it's yours once you
testify for the narcs."

"Okay, but I want to get out of here right now."

"Okay, kid. I'll ride up the driveway with you and move
my truck."

I let him watch me tuck the .38 into my belt. Wasn't it
Mao who said that political power comes from the barrel
of a gun? We got in his little yellow car and drove up to
the Landcruiser. I backed it off enough for him to get by,
and he roared out onto the highway the way drivers of
such sportscars seem to feel they must drive—with a lot
of engine and brakes. His tires squealed as he raced
away.

I drove down to the house and made a copy of the tape,
which I put in the shed with the drugs I'd been accumu-
lating over the past few days. I examined my gun cabinet.
The lock was broken, but the only items that had been
removed were the pistol and its ammunition. The long
guns were still there. A more proficient killer would have

used a shotgun on me, but Billy was never a shotgun user, having refused to learn the gunner's craft from his father. I doubted if he knew one shotgun from another. Or one pistol from another, for that matter. He'd found my old .38 and was going to do the job with that. But he hadn't. And when I had my chance, I hadn't either. I'd wanted to, but I hadn't. I wasn't sure why.

I put the pistol in its holster and put both under the front seat of the Landcruiser, then I drove downtown and found the chief walking from the post office, an armful of mail clutched under his arm.

"Say," I said, "I always wondered about this. Do you guys get junk mail, too? Or is it just us civilians? I can't believe that all that stuff is legitimate police business."

"I could carry the legitimate stuff in my shirt pocket," growled the chief. He did not look happy to see me as I fell into step beside him. I dug out the original tape.

"Here," I said. "I think you'll find this worth listening to right away. Emphasis on right away. Capital letters— RIGHT AWAY." I put the tape in the chief's shirt pocket and followed him into the police station. Helen Viera was at the desk.

"Helen," said the chief, "find that tape recorder we've got, will you? It's around here somewhere."

I gave her an encouraging smile and followed the chief back into his private office. "Gee," I said, "you mean you're actually going to do it? You're actually going to play it? I don't even have to pay you or kiss your shoes or anything?"

"You can lick my boots later if you want to," said the chief, unloading his mail onto the desk. Helen came in, put a small cassette recorder on the desk, and went out again.

"It'll take about half an hour," I said, sitting down on

one of the hard chairs the taxpayers of Edgartown had purchased for their men in blue. "I think you may find it interesting."

I watched enviously while the chief stoked up his pipe. He shook out the match, popped the tape into the machine, and sat back in his chair. I observed that it was nicely padded, unlike mine. A professional perk, no doubt.

When the tape was done, the chief opened his eyes and looked at me. "Did he really point a gun at you?"

"Indeed he did. My own."

"I think a good lawyer could shred this tape faster than Colonel North, but I guess we'd better have a talk with Billy anyway, just to let him know we've got an eye on him. How can you be so sure that a big bust is actually coming down soon?"

"I have a source in Boston. An old pro news guy who knows how to dig. If you want to know how good he really is, I can tell you that the bust is scheduled for tonight."

"Jesus Christ! Don't say that!" The chief involuntarily looked around the empty room in case any invisible people were listening. They weren't. Then his expression changed. "You didn't get that from anybody down here, then?"

"No."

"Okay." He stared at me. "How upset was Billy when he left you? Upset enough to get another gun? His daddy's got plenty of them."

"I don't know."

"I'll have somebody stay with you, if you want. Just until we find Billy."

I expressed shock. "One of your summer rent-a-cops? No, thanks! I have a hard enough time looking after myself, let alone somebody who can't grow hair on his face!"

"Suit yourself, but be careful. I got trouble enough with traffic and drunks. I don't need any more corpses showing up, not even yours."

"Maybe you won't have to find Billy. Maybe he'll come in just like he said he would."

The chief scowled. "And maybe I'm the king of Siam."

I drove to Oak Bluffs and returned Bonzo's equipment to his mother. No, I said, I hadn't recorded anything interesting. That was too bad, she said. Bonzo would be disappointed. As I left her, I noticed that it was clouding up in the west. Red sky at night?

I thought of Zee, then remembered that she'd be on duty in the emergency ward. I also remembered the laugh she'd shared with the young doctor there. I got into the Landcruiser and drove deliberately back to Edgartown, wearing my hat all the way and ignoring the lengthening line of traffic behind me. At the head of every long line of traffic there is a man wearing a hat—Hatman. I was Hatman today, irritating people behind me because I was irritated by my memory of Zee and the doctor.

I drove to Eelpond, dug out my gloves and clam basket, and spent two hours digging steamers as the clouds gathered. It was getting muggy. Back at the Landcruiser I got my five-gallon lidded plastic bucket that I'd found on South Beach almost as good as new, filled it half full of salt water, and dumped the clams in. Snapping the lid on the bucket and jamming everything back into the Landcruiser I tried to imagine how the clams would taste, but imagining instead how good Zee would taste. Delicious, I reckoned.

Thus occupied with thoughts divine, I drove home, parked, and was lifting my bucket of clams out of the Landcruiser just as Billy Martin stepped around the corner of the house, a shotgun at his shoulder.

"Good-bye, asshole," said Billy, and he pulled the trigger.

* 18 *

Most of the shot went into the plastic bucket, where it mangled already doomed clams. Some of the rest hit various parts of me. Pleased to discover that I could still move, I did so, throwing the gaping bucket at Billy and running around the corner of the house as Billy pumped another round into the firing chamber. Curiously, I even had time to identify the gun—George Martin's pump Remington .20 gauge, beside which I had sat in more than one blind while George and I hunted for ducks and geese.

With a full head of steam, I ran into the woods, thinking that George's Remington held only three shots and that at the most Billy could have only two shots left. Just then, he let the second one go, and the top of me started going faster than my legs and I fell down. But then I was up again and running quite well, I thought, all things considered. Leaves around me fluttered and fell as I heard a third shot far behind me. The sound of shot rattled through the bushes.

I was still alive! Thorns snagged me and branches whipped my face and clutched at me, but I ran on, heart pounding, lungs pumping. I ran into a tree and fell down. I got up and went on. Glancing back, I saw no Billy in sight. But I ran on some more, noticing now that I was bleeding in many places, the blood oozing through my clothes.

It came to me that the only reason I was still alive was that foolish, murderous Billy, never having liked hunting or fishing with his old man and therefore knowing little of either sport, had loaded his father's shotgun with birdshot instead of buckshot. The bigger the number, the smaller the shot, but Billy apparently had figured the bigger the number the bigger the shot. Thus I was fairly well peppered, but still alive and mobile. Billy was not very good at killing people, but he was getting better. At least he was using a shotgun now. Next time he'd probably get the right slugs in it.

Somewhere ahead was the highway, and not too far away there was a neighboring farmhouse. I needed both the police and the hospital. I came to the highway and stopped suddenly in the trees. What if Billy was cruising along that stretch, knowing that I would probably come out there just as, in fact, I was doing? Something had popped inside of Billy, making him no longer just a killer in secret. Now he'd come out into the open; he'd gone public with his violence.

I stuck my bleeding face out of the trees and surveyed the scene. My own driveway was a quarter of a mile away. As I looked toward it, a red sportscar came out, paused, and turned toward me. Beginning to hurt now and feeling a bit woozy, I lay down in the scrub oak. The car approached, slowed, slowed more, then eased on by, its exhaust murmuring expensively. Leaking blood, I tried to look like fallen leaves. Billy's face looked at me but saw nothing, and the car went on down the road. It occurred to me that Billy must have hidden the car behind the shed while he waited in ambush.

I wondered whose car it was and thought I remembered seeing a little car like that parked on the dock near the *Bluefin.* Tim Mello's car, maybe? My head was fuzzy. I decided to get up and find help, but found getting up harder than I expected. I was probably losing more blood than I could spare and was perhaps going into shock. This thought lifted me to my feet and sent me staggering out into the highway.

What if Billy turned around and came back? Too late now. A car came by and I put up both hands and waved for it to stop. The driver, seeing a wild-eyed and bloody man dressed in torn clothes, accelerated past and fled on down the road. I staggered along the road, tried and failed to stop two more cars, the drivers of which shared the alarm of the first driver who had passed me. Feeling tired, I sat down just as a girl driving a pickup stopped beside me. She was a suntanned girl wearing shorts, sandals, and a blue shirt. She jumped out and knelt beside me.

"Can I move you?"

I considered the question fizzily, then nodded. She put an arm under me and got me up and into the pickup.

"I'm going to bleed all over your car," I said, feeling apologetic. I saw that I'd already bloodied her clothes.

"Don't worry about it," she said. She wrapped me in a beach towel and drove off.. As we sped up the road, I thought I saw the red sportscar coming back, and I slid down out of sight a bit. The girl glanced at me and stepped on the gas.

I faded away then and only eased back awake as they were wheeling me into the emergency room on a stretcher. I heard a startled voice:

"Jeff!"

Zee. Still on duty and obviously surprised to see me.

"Hi," I said. "It's me."

Her lovely face appeared. Beside it was the face of the young doctor. I rolled my head away, looking for the girl who'd brought me in. She was gone. The Good Samaritan. I requested a blessing for her from whatever gods there might be, then rolled my head back and smiled up at Zee. "I have a problem, folks," I said.

"Don't talk," said Zee.

"I think it looks worse than it is," I said. "It's birdshot, I think, and I've got some of it in front and back, both. But I don't think any of it went deep enough to do any serious damage to my gizzard or anything else inside there. I may be a little short of blood, though."

Zee faded away, then came back. Other faces appeared and disappeared. There was a muted roaring in my ears that came and went with the faces. Time apparently passed.

"I think he's all right," said a voice I took to be the young doctor's. "These appear to be superficial wounds. We'll be a while picking out the pellets, though."

I felt the prick of a needle and then was looking at the ceiling. There was a tube in my arm and I was covered with a sheet dotted with red spots. Seepage. I rolled my head and there was Zee, sitting beside me with a worried look in her eyes and the suggestion that tears had been responsible for her slightly smudged mascara.

"We've got a problem," I said.

"Oh, thank God! You're awake!" She reached out a hand and touched my shoulder.

"Gosh and gee whiz," I said. "If I'd known that this was all it took to make you concerned about my well-being, I'd have done it sooner."

"Be careful how you talk," she said. "You're at my

mercy. I'll whack you on a bullet hole if you don't behave and keep a civil tongue in your head." She pressed my shoulder, then got up. "Stay right there. I'll get the doctor."

The doctor was young and serious. He was also the same one I'd seen laughing with Zee. He listened to my heart, checked my pulse and blood pressure, took my temperature, and then nodded. "We've given you some shots and some blood and dug most of the lead out of you, and it looks like you're going to be okay, Mr. Jackson." He smiled, then was serious again. Too serious a guy for Zee, I decided.

"Are the police here?" I asked.

"They came and left. It seems that tonight something big is happening that's keeping them very busy. They asked me to call them when you were awake. They want to talk to you about this."

Yes, tonight was drug-bust night. It seemed a distant sort of business. "Where am I right now? Am I still in the emergency ward?"

"No. We've got you in a room down the hall in the hospital. Why?"

"What time is it? How long have I been in here?"

"It's about ten o'clock. They brought you in about six. Why do you ask?"

"Because I don't think it's a good idea for me to be here. The guy who shot me—Billy Martin, just for the record—" Zee's eyes widened, the doctor's didn't. "Anyway, Billy is a little wacky, I think. Maybe he's taking something to give him courage or something, but in any case he tried to kill me right in my own front yard, then he drove up and down the highway in broad daylight looking for me so he could finish me off. Finally he must have figured it out that

I was either lying in the woods or I'd made it to the hospital. He'd have checked the woods while there was still light, and when he didn't find me there, he'd expect to find me here. And being the loony that he is, I wouldn't be surprised if he came right in here after me. He's just crazy enough."

"I'll call the police," said the doctor, and he hurried from the room. Zee was at the windows pulling the curtains shut. I tried to sit up. Made it. The needle in my arm pricked me. I took it out.

"Where are my clothes?"

"In the locker. Stay right there." Zee crossed the room and went toward the door. There was something odd about her voice.

"What is it?" I asked.

"I can see the parking lot from your window. I think I just saw Billy Martin get out of a car." She pointed at me. "Stay, Fang."

Then she was gone.

* 19 *

I had my legs over the edge of the bed when she came back. My skin felt on fire. "It's him, all right," said Zee, coming in as quickly as she'd gone. She went to a locker, dug around, and flung me my bloody clothes. "Stay on the bed. Dress. Be quiet!"

She pushed the bed into the hall. We rounded a corner, then another. At the next to the last room she wheeled me inside. It was a four-bed ward with another occupant asleep in a far bed. Inside, Zee yanked an existing bed out and replaced it with mine, with me still aboard.

"Dress, damn it!" Her voice was a hiss. She swept the curtains around me and I heard her exiting with the bed mine had just replaced. I struggled into my clothes. All of me hurt. I oozed my feet into my shoes and slid off the bed.

Right onto the floor. No zip in the old bod. I sat there awhile, then got myself together and pulled myself up, using the bed as a support. I sat on it, resting, panting. Then Zee was back again.

"Billy's headed for your room. I guess he got the room number from somebody in emergency. When he gets to your room, he won't find you. He'll either drop the whole

167

thing or he'll start looking for you. It'll take him time to get here and maybe by then the police will have arrived."

"And maybe they won't," I said.

"That's right, so we're leaving. My car's out back."

"Fine." I stood up from the bed, swayed, and felt her arm around me.

"Come on, then. Lean on me. Put your arm over my shoulder."

I did. We staggered down the hall toward the door, then outside. I glanced back and thought I saw blood where we'd walked. I was apparently leaking a bit and leaving a trail.

"Come on, come on," said Zee. "Stop walking in circles."

I tried walking straight. Women are terribly strong. I was remembering seeing them shopping, a baby on a hip, another child dragging on a skirt and mom pushing a carriage weighing three or four tons. Could dad manage all that? Probably not. Thus I admired Zee as she hefted me across the parking lot and into her Jeep. It was dark and windy. Lightning glowed in the west. I noticed that her rod was on the roof rack. Had she really been practicing without me?

"Marry me," I said. "In forty years or so I'm going to need somebody to carry me around like this all the time. I think you can do the job."

"Shut up," said Zee.

I slouched in the seat, feeling woozy. "Where are we going?"

"Away from here." As we pulled out of the main parking lot, Zee looked to the right and cursed. I followed her gaze and saw a red sportscar easing toward us. "Blast and drat," said Zee. "That looks like the car Billy was driving."

At that moment the car passed beneath a streetlight. It did indeed look like the car I'd seen Billy driving after he'd shotgunned me. I slid down in the seat. "I thought he was inside the hospital," I said.

"He was! I saw him! He must have ducked out again as soon as he found your room empty! If he recognizes my Jeep, he may put two and two together." At the end of the drive, she turned toward the oncoming headlights. Smart Zee. Billy would be partially blinded by the lights and might not recognize her Jeep.

Billy passed us. I grunted my way back up onto the seat and looked back. Son of a bitch! He was turning around in the hospital driveway.

"Step on it," I said. "I think he's on to us!"

"Madre!" Zee hit the gas and we scooted around the corner. Ahead were three choices of travel: left toward East Chop, straight ahead, or right into the emergency room parking lot. Zee turned off her headlights and went straight ahead. She took her next right and swept toward the lobster hatchery.

Zoom. Through the night. Trees whipped by, dimly lit by scattered streetlights. Scary but interesting. Behind us—nothing. Zee sped on, over a hill into a shallow hollow and up the other side and into another hollow. The stars reeled in the sky. I felt pretty good. Behind us I still saw no lights. Billy had guessed wrong about our flight plan. Zee made a hard right turn through a stop sign and flicked on the lights.

"Quo vadis?" I inquired.

"My place. I'll call the cops from there. I think we've lost our tail, as they say in the movies."

"You drive good," I said.

"Shut up and concentrate on not bleeding."

We came to the blinker on the Edgartown–Vineyard Haven Road, crossed and went on. Then suddenly there were no more stars. Clouds had covered them, blowing in from the west. The trees flipped by on either side of the road, dark against a dark sky. Still no tail. Billy had definitely gone off somewhere else. I wondered where. I wondered how deep shotgun pellets went in. I wondered if they'd gotten them all out or whether I'd be carrying some of them around for the rest of my life, however long that might be. Not too long, at the rate I was going today. I asked Zee about the pellets.

"From what I could see, they went in a half inch to an inch. We got most of them out, but you'll probably get to keep the rest. Just like that shrapnel you carry around. As far as I know, none of the shot went deep enough to touch anything vital. You hurt, but you'll be okay." She gave me a quick look. "Mostly he got you around the edges. The doctor found that curious."

"Clams," I said.

"What?"

I told her about the clam bucket taking the first blast. "Greater love hath no clam than he will lay down his life for his clammer."

"Maybe you should lay off shellfish as a gesture of appreciation."

We drove past the airport to West Tisbury and turned left toward Chilmark. Behind us headlights appeared. Zee stepped on the gas.

"Does he know where you live?" I asked.

"Not that I know of."

The rain began as we passed the general store. Off toward Gay Head, lightning glittered. A bit later we could hear the thunder. A summer storm was walking down

Vineyard Sound from the west, filling the sky with glowing lights and jagged flashes. I don't like thunderstorms. They scare me. But I liked this one. It would make it harder for crazy Billy to find his way around. Red sky at night, Jackson's delight.

We found Zee's road and drove to the house. By then the rain was beating down and the thunder was crashing. A fine bolt of lightning lanced down to the north of us, and I counted. Eight seconds. A mile and a half or so. Close enough to be impressive, but not close enough to be dangerous. My kind of lightning.

"Stay here," said Zee. She opened the door of the Jeep and ran, ducking, through the rain. Why do we duck when we run through the rain? We get just as wet. Zee reached her porch, went into the house, and turned on a light, then came back with an umbrella. She got me and we walked, ducking, to the house.

Zee walked me right into her bedroom.

"Get undressed and get into bed."

"Try to control yourself," I said. "I'm a wounded man."

"Ha, ha," she said. But then she smiled. "Get undressed. Remember, I've already seen your naked bod stretched out on the operating table at the hospital. You have no secrets from me."

"But you have some from me."

"I don't think you're up to discovery right now. I'll get you something hot to drink."

She went out and came back after a bit with a teapot and two cups. I was still sitting there, thinking. As I raised my hand for the cup, the lights went out. I could see Zee outlined against the window where outside the sky glowed and thunder muttered. I heard her put down the teapot and cups, then she walked out of the room and I could hear a drawer open and close. Then a light danced beyond the bedroom door and she came back in cupping a thick candle and carrying two others. She lit these and the bedroom brightened, soft, yellow, and glimmering in that lovely light that only candles can give. She served my tea.

"Romance." She smiled.

It was herb tea laced with rum. I scalded a tonsil and the next time blew the surface cool before I drank.

"You're a good cook," I said. "I'm glad I came."

"You bring out the mother in me."

"I do have a boyish charm, but behind this baby face and beneath this ivory skin lives a truly manly man, full of lust and mad passions I'm only able to control by dint of an iron will, which is another of my manly traits. I should warn you, however, that my superego is eaten alive by my id when I'm in the presence of a champion tea maker of your general configuration."

"You must be feeling better," she said. "Before you get so excited that you fall down on the floor, I think I'll make that phone call to the police. They can send someone out here to protect us from each other."

"Good thinking." I sipped my tea, feeling not really too great. Then I put the cup down and lay back on the bed. Zee came back.

"Guess what?"

"What?"

"The phone's out, too."

I lay there and looked at her ceiling. The candles cast a wavy light that threw faint shadows everywhere. Quite lovely.

"I don't suppose you have a gun of some sort lying around."

"I don't know anything about guns and I don't have any. I'm barely beginning to learn about fishing."

"It probably doesn't make any difference. Billy's not the type to wander around in weather bad as this. Not at night, at least. It's hard to see your hand in front of your face."

"Yes. Which means it's just as hard for the cops to see Billy."

"They'll find him. There's more of them than of him." I tried to sound confident.

"I'd think so, too, if he was driving his own car. But you saw that car he was in tonight. It wasn't that little yellow M.G. he usually drives. The police will be looking for the M.G., I imagine, not for the red car he's driving now."

I sat up and carefully put my feet on the floor. Outside, thunder and lightning cracked together and the rain doubled its intensity. "I think we may have a problem," I said. "Billy doesn't know where you live, but . . ."

"But it's not a secret. He could find out. . . ."

"How?"

She was quick. "If I were Billy, I'd phone the hospital claiming to be a police officer looking for Zee Madeiras's home. If I were a nurse, I'd probably give the information without thinking too much about it."

I moved and winced and saw Zee wince when she saw me wince. I tried to think straight. "You didn't mention seeing Billy carrying a shotgun in the hospital, so he's probably got one of his daddy's target pistols or even my pistol from the Landcruiser where I was stupid enough to leave it. He likes that gun. He almost shot me with it earlier in the day."

"I think we'd better get out of here," said Zee. "We ought to find some cops and let them watch over you. I don't think my fishing rod is a match for his six-shooter!"

I waved a finger in the air. "Peace, peace. Even if he finds out where you live, he still doesn't know I'm with you. Besides, finding a cop tonight might be hard. Most of them are probably out drug busting. Anyhow, if we go driving back down island looking for policemen, Billy might just spot us on the road. . . ."

"He knows my Jeep. He passed us, then turned around, remember?"

"He may suspect that I'm with you, but he doesn't know."

"Great. A suspicious madman. That's very comforting, Jefferson. You're a real psychologist. Now I don't know what to do! Stay and get killed or leave and get killed? Some choice!"

I tried to put myself into Billy's head. What would I do? Where would I go? How would I act?

Zee was clearer in the brain than I was. "We're getting out of here. We'll hide out up at Lobsterville by Dogfish Bar till morning. They should have him by then." She headed for the kitchen. "I'll fix a thermos of coffee and some sandwiches to see us through."

"Good idea." I was relieved by having a decision made by Zee, since I was too muddleheaded to make one myself.

When she'd fixed the food and coffee, she helped me through the rain to the Jeep and we went off. "I'm sorry about the discomfort you're going to be in, Jefferson," she said, "but you'll survive it. We'll have food and drink and I'll keep the heater on as often as we need it. Maybe you can even get some sleep." She sounded like a nurse—kind but firm. Realistic. Men like to think of themselves as the realists, but they're wrong. Women are the gender of reality. They live in a concrete world of men, children, and feelings while men entertain themselves with great abstractions—money, power, fantasies of heroism.

I thought of a question. "Dogfish Bar? How do you know about Dogfish Bar? I thought you were just a neophyte fisherperson. Neophytes don't know about Dogfish Bar."

"What do you know about what I know? I keep my ears open, mister. Dogfish Bar is where they catch the bass. Right up there beyond Lobsterville. Billy will never think of looking for us there."

Who could tell where mad Billy might think of looking? "Have you been hanging around with some up-island fisherman when I'm not around?"

"None of your business."

True. I felt sulky nevertheless, and frowned into the darkness.

We passed through Chilmark and entered Gay Head, home of the lovely clay cliffs and the made-in-Japan Indian souvenirs sold to tourists by Gay Headers. I don't really like Gay Head because I can never find a free parking place up there and they charge for using the toilets. When I'm king of the world I'm going to ban pay toilets as an affront to civilization.

In the darkness the wind shook the trees, the rain began to thin, and the sky to the east flashed and glittered as the thunderstorm moved off toward Nantucket. Zee took the Lobsterville road.

"All right," she said, slowing down, "where is it?"

"Where's what?"

"Where's the road to Dogfish Bar? You're the big fisherman around here. Tell me where to turn. I know I turn somewhere, but I don't know where."

Gee whiz and gollee. Maybe she wasn't hanging out with

some up-island fisherman after all! I smiled into the darkness and my sulk went away. I told her where to turn—first left toward Gay Head light, then right. Ahead, all was darkness. No electricity up island, yet. The road was sand and full of dips and rises and holes and ruts. When we got opposite Dogfish Bar, we pulled off and parked in the beach grass and bushes. Our headlights illuminated the thin trail leading north over the dunes.

"Follow that," I said, "and when you feel the water over your knees you'll know you've gone too far. Come back onto the beach and make your cast and it'll land on Dogfish Bar."

Zee punched out the headlights and turned off the engine. Lightning danced in the east and thunder was faint. She found a soft rock station and the music eased out of the speakers. Personally I only listen to folk, classical, and country, but I'm a broadminded guy so I'd listen to this without complaint because I was her guest. I explained this to Zee. She expressed great admiration for my character and gracious ways.

After a while we had some coffee and food and she asked me about bass fishing. I told her how I did it—fresh squid from Menemsha, night fishing only. You make your cast and then let the tide take the squid across the shallows. If a bass takes it, it feels nothing at all like a bluefish and you can tell the difference right away. You have to let the big ones run, and they'll head for the rocks if there are any, and you have to play them a long time sometimes before you begin to get them in close and then all the way in.

I told her how they were getting pretty scarce along the East Coast and that I didn't fish for them anymore, myself, except now and then, for a change, and only if I really wanted to eat one, and then only a little illegal one because I wanted the big ones to go back home and lay eggs and build the bass population up again.

I asked Zee if she'd noticed my Hemingway imitation, but she said she hadn't. Then she asked me if I'd ever wondered why George's nitroglycerin pills hadn't worked better on our run from Cape Pogue to Edgartown and I said I hadn't because I'd forgotten George mentioning it. And after I thought about it now, I said that maybe it would be a good idea to have the pills checked out, just in case George needed them again sometime. She said she'd take care of it.

While I was thinking about the pills and how comfortable I was, I went to sleep. As I drifted away I remember seeing the horizon off to the east glow with distant lightning. The wind still blew strong around the Jeep, but the rain had stopped.

When I woke up, the storm was gone, the sky was clear, and the sun was shining. I blinked into its rays and saw a red M.G. sportscar swaying and splashing up the road toward us, moving fast.

* 20 *

"Wake up!" I shook Zee and she was instantly awake. "There!" I pointed. She saw and reached for the ignition key. As the motor roared, I slid out the door. I felt as if my skin was tearing away.

"What are you doing! Get in here!" She clawed after me.

"No. This road dead-ends, and he's between us and the highway. He wants me. I'll let him see me, and when he comes after me, you go for the police. Don't let him get too close to you because he might just shoot you in passing!"

"No!"

"Yes!"

I slammed the door and threw a look at the sportscar. It was only a hundred yards away, bouncing through pools of rainwater and throwing sand and mud into the air. I trotted around into plain sight and began a limping lope up the trail toward the dunes. I dared not pause to look behind me, but I heard the scream of the sportscar's engine as Billy turned after me and tried to drive up the trail.

But the ground was too rough for the low-slung M.G., and as I gimped over the first dune I heard the whine of spinning wheels. Then I was running down the far side of the dune, hurting, and then I was climbing the second dune separating the beach from the road. As I topped it, Billy must have reached the top of the first dune, for I heard the crack of his pistol. I leaped down the far side of the dune, tripped and fell, got up, and ran.

I reached the beach and ran east toward Lobsterville. By now Zee should be on her way for help. I wondered how long I could run. I had never been much of a runner even when young and frisky. I was the guy who got a stitch in his side after a quarter of a mile and couldn't stand it. Now I was thirty-five and not frisky at all, and I had shotgun pellets and holes of same all over my body and I was having a hard time standing them.

But fear is a wonderful motivator, as I'd found out in Vietnam when I'd done a lot of running first in one direction then another, never making much progress for long, but too scared to stop. Behind me, over the sound of the waves splashing against the shingle beach, Billy's pistol popped again. Again he missed, but to my right some pebbles rattled. It's hard to hit anything with a pistol under the best of circumstances. When you're half crazy and are running and out of breath and shooting at a moving target, it's even harder.

I ran on. Pretty soon Billy would figure out that he had to run me down in order to get close enough to shoot me. If I could keep running, maybe he'd give up and go home. Maybe I could run him into the ground. Why not? Stranger things have happened.

A hammer hit my left thigh and the leg collapsed and I fell, skidding through pebbles. Not good. I tried to get up, but the leg wouldn't work. I rolled over and looked back. Billy was running toward me, pistol in hand. The bastard had shot me!

He came running up and stopped, panting, and looked down at me. Suddenly, far behind him, I saw Zee come onto the beach. She had her fishing rod.

"You turd," said Billy, huffing and puffing. "You motherfucker. You chickenshit."

I threw a rock at him. He ducked and laughed.

"Get away!" I yelled at Zee. "Run!"

Billy turned and saw her, then turned back. "I'll get her next. You first, turd."

He took a breath to steady his arm and raised the pistol as Zee made her cast. The diamond jig arched through the air and slapped down over his face, and she lay back on the rod and set the triple hook in his cheek. Billy screamed and staggered backward, clawing at his face. The pistol went off, then flew away into the surf. Zee backed and jerked on the rod, and Billy tore at the jig, blood bursting through his hands.

Zee had twenty-pound test line and forty-five pound test leader, and neither was going to break. She backed up the beach while Billy, screaming, reeled after her. Then he fell, and I saw the jig tear loose and fly away. Zee dropped the rod and came running, her fillet knife glittering in her hand. Billy staggered up, blood pouring from his torn face. He saw Zee, slipped on the bloody pebbles beneath him, gave an awful cry and plunged away toward the dunes, scrambling for cover like the wounded animal he was. Zee, her face contorted, swerved, running, toward him, then turned back to me. Billy thrashed up and over the dunes and was gone.

Then Zee had me in her arms, and she was crying and so was I.

By the time she got me back to the Jeep, the M.G. was gone. There were tire marks deep in the beach grass and a smear of oil, too. He'd done his oil pan a bad turn before he'd gotten away. I didn't think he'd drive too far before his engine let go.

We stopped at the first house we came to, and Zee went in to call the police. The phone was working, and we were promised an ambulance and a police escort to the hospital. My leg was well awake by now and hurting quite a bit. It wasn't bleeding too badly, though, which meant the bullet had missed the bigger arteries and veins. Zee gave me aspirin and held my hand.

The house had a fine view, and I could see the fishing boats and early departing yachts moving out of Menemsha Gut to begin their morning cruises. Several were small swordfishermen with long pulpits. Probably headed for the swordfishing grounds south of Nomans Land, I thought. Then I thought I saw the *Bluefin* heading out as well. But the ambulance came just then, and Zee helped me get into it and then got in back with me and we pulled away toward Oak Bluffs.

As we approached Beetlebung Corner we came to a near stop. I sat up and saw that there were police cars clustered around the red M.G. A young officer waved us by. I didn't see Billy in anyone's custody, but maybe they'd already taken him off. Maybe not.

"If they don't have him now, they'll get him soon," I said to Zee. I was quite wrong, as things turned out, but I was sincere.

Neither my ambulance nor my police escort sounded a siren on the way, but I got to the hospital anyway and was hustled once again into the emergency room. The staff affected dismay, claiming I was taking up more time than any single person merited. From this I gathered that I was not as seriously shot as I might have been. This proved indeed to be the case, for after due procedure I found myself again in a clean white bed, another bit of lead removed from my flesh.

"How are you feeling?" asked Zee.

I put on my manly smile. She rolled her eyes to heaven, then kissed my forehead and took my hand and held it and I really didn't feel too bad at all. After a while I went to sleep.

When I woke up I noticed a cop at the door. He glanced at me, then disappeared. A moment later he was back and the chief walked in.

"How you doing?"

"Not bad. Why the armed guard?"

"That's to protect the nurses."

"Sure."

"Billy's still on the loose. We missed him."

Not good, Kemo Sabe. "I saw his car up in Chilmark. He couldn't have gotten far, and anybody who'd have seen him would remember him because of his face. He must still be up there somewhere."

"We've got a lot of men scouring the area. If he's there, we'll find him."

"If he's there?"

"There was a lady up there walking. Her morning constitutional. Billy passed her in the M.G. She said it was making an awful noise and finally stopped a ways behind her. A man with a bleeding face got out, and about that time a car came up, stopped, and picked him up, then turned around and drove away."

"Which way?"

"Back toward Beetlebung Corner. After that, she didn't notice."

I put a map of the Vineyard in my head. The island looks small, but there are over a hundred square miles of it. I couldn't even guess how many miles of road and driveways wound through the trees and grapevines. From Beetlebung Corner alone you could take three paved roads leading away from Gay Head—Menemsha Cross Road, Middle Road, or South Road. A car could be a lot of places.

"What kind of car was it that picked him up? A black Caddy, maybe?"

"She didn't know. Tan. Two doors. Newish. She doesn't know one car from another since they stopped putting brand names on them. Lots of times I don't either, for that matter."

"Do you have any other good news for me?"

"Nope."

"How did the big bust go?"

He rolled an oath out of his mouth and ran a hand through his thinning hair. "Small fry only. The big guys got tipped again."

"Fred Sylvia and group?"

He looked at me hard. "What do you know about Sylvia?"

"I'm an ex-big-city copper, remember. I got contacts. I heard the name in a couple of places."

He was not at all amused. "You know a lot for somebody who isn't supposed to know anything at all. Being so smart, you could be the guy who tipped Sylvia."

"Sure I did. I phoned him from the hospital while they were picking number seven-and-a-half shot out of me."

The chief shook out a cigarette and thrust it at me. "Smoke?" When I shook my head, he stuck the cigarette in his own mouth and lit up. "I've had a bad night and it looks like I'll be having a bad day, too. It makes me grouchy." He looked at the cigarette in his hand. "I should give these up." Instead, he put the cigarette back in his mouth and inhaled deeply.

"How did you miss Sylvia?"

"Whoever tipped them before, tipped them again, so he was gone before we could get there. We think we know what Sylvia was doing and how he did it, but we needed his computer and its programs to make a case."

"You mean that computer on his desk in his home office?"

"How did you know about that?"

"I visited him once a few days ago. How did his system work?"

"We got all this from the DEA guys before we began the raids last night. According to them, Fred Sylvia is a leader in a drug-trafficking business that covers a lot of the Northeast. He's been running the organization from his home office just like you might run a legitimate business, and at the same time he's kept his legitimate interests in Brunner International. Because he knows Brunner International's schedules for imports and exports, he's been able to add drug shipments to legitimate cargoes and hide them in his computer inventories. That's how he got the stuff into the States. Pretty slick.

"Then, being the good businessman that he is, and he *is* good at business, he set up an organization he called the Janus Public Service Corporation. He entered agreements with other drug dealers, bought their lists of customers, provided paid vacations for his employees, gave some free apartments and cars, and paid them all good salaries.

We're told the salaries range up to five thousand dollars a week, and that the corporation sold several hundred kilos of cocaine and over a ton of marijuana last year, to say nothing of other drugs.

"He paid out thousands in salaries, and paid himself a hefty one, too, as corporation president. But he was always fair with his employees, so there was a lot of loyalty throughout the organization. If we'd gotten him, though, we could also have nailed him for income tax evasion, because naturally he never reported the Janus Corporation salary."

"How'd you get onto him?"

"Not me, them, the DEA. Oh, sooner or later there's a breakdown in the system. Somebody talked and fingered a higher-up. The DEA agreed not to prosecute if the guy would tell all. And he did tell what he knew and so the DEA guys got more names and made more deals. The standard stuff: they let off the small fry to get at the bigger ones and finally learned what I just told you."

"But without the computer records, all they've got is rumors."

"They'd have liked the *Bluefin,* too. They figure the Janus outfit used it to ferry drugs here and there when the boat was supposed to be out on long-range fishing trips, and they figured they might find some evidence aboard that would add to their case. And of course they would have liked to have Sylvia and some of his associates in hand, to ask some questions so they could compare stories and maybe get somebody to break and talk."

"Somebody like Tim Mello, the guy who captains the *Bluefin.*" I'd liked Tim, but who says the baddies are unpleasant? They only make their money differently than

most of us. Aside from that, they're pretty much like
everybody else. Some you'll like, some you won't."

"That was one of the names. And a guy named Leon Jax
who provides whatever muscle Sylvia needs."

"And the whole thing went bust."

"A busted bust. Us locals helped the big guys find their
way around so they wouldn't get lost, but it was really their
game. They had warrants for Sylvia's house and boat and
they wanted his car, but all they found was the car. The
house was empty and the *Bluefin* was gone. The guys on
the docks told them that Tim Mello had said he was bound
swordfishing with Sylvia. Of course they left last night and
we didn't find out where till this morning. So all we got for
our efforts were some local dealers and users who probably didn't get their stuff from Sylvia anyway."

"Where was the car? A black Caddy, I take it."

The chief snubbed out his cigarette. "That's the second
time you've mentioned a black Caddy. Why?"

"I saw Leon driving one once. Where did you find the
car? Down at the *Bluefin*'s dock, I'd guess, and clean as a
cat's whiskers."

"Yep. Right where he'd have left it if he was going
swordfishing for a day or two."

"I imagine you've got the Coast Guard looking for the
Bluefin out around the swordfishing grounds."

"They're looking, but I doubt if they'll do much finding." The chief got up. "I've blabbed enough. There'll be
a guard outside, just in case. Just wanted to let you know
what was happening."

"Did you search Mrs. Sylvia's car?" I asked.

He paused as he was stepping toward the door. "No, we
didn't find it. Or her, either." He frowned at me.

"I think you'll find her car up in Menemsha. A tan

two-door Buick. A car like the one that picked Billy up this morning."

"Why do you think it's in Menemsha?"

"Because I think I saw the *Bluefin* pull out of Menemsha Gut this morning about the time it would have taken Billy to get to Beetlebung Corner and someone else to drive him to Menemsha."

"A tan two-door? You're sure?"

"I saw her driving one last week. If I were a guessing man, which I am, I'd guess that she picked Billy up and they went for a cruise in the *Bluefin*."

"I'll get on the horn." He slapped his hat on his head. "There are men up there who can check it out."

"You might also tell the Coast Guard to look for the boat someplace else than on the swordfishing grounds."

"Believe it or not, I already thought of that!" He frowned, gestured good-bye, and left.

Not much later, there was a commotion outside my door. Someone saying he damned well would see me and the policeman doubting it. After a bit, the policeman stuck his head in and said, "There's a guy named Quinn out here. Says you're supposed to take him fishing this afternoon."

"Send him in."

Quinn came in looking very neat in one of the Brooks Brothers suits he favors. It's his way of proving that not all reporters have to look seedy. He gave me a sour look.

"Don't tell me. You're reneging on the deal. Jesus Christ, Jackson, have you no shame?"

"None. If I did, I certainly wouldn't associate with you."

"When are they going to let you out of here?"

"The sooner the better."

"Well, you're not wriggling out from our deal. I'll be

PHILIP R. CRAIG

expecting a call as soon as you're mobile and I'll be down before you can change your mind. You owe me a blue-fishing trip to Wasque!"

"Stop nagging. I'm a sick man. You'll get your trip."

After a bit, Quinn went away. He was a friend of long standing. A man with a tough mouth but a soft heart, like a lot in his trade.

* 21 *

I really loathe being in a hospital. The food is dull, you can't have beer, everything is clean and smells funny. People are so nice so much of the time that you're almost relieved when one of them isn't. Of course, the knowledge that Zee was in close proximity much of the time did serve as a salve to my psyche.

She dropped in while she was working and visited when she wasn't and one day brought in some rolled flounder stuffed with mushrooms and crab. There was a sauce with dill in it and wild rice and baby peas on the side and a smuggled bottle of chilled Moselle, which the on-duty folks were pleased to ignore while we devoured the feast.

"It's the turning point," I said afterward. "My will to live has been revitalized. I know that soon I'll walk in the sun again, hear the crash of waves on the rockbound coast, feel the wind on my face! You've saved me!"

"I've saved every poor soul who's had to listen to you bitch and moan, you mean," said Zee, gathering up china and silverware and sticking everything back into her picnic basket. "They're letting you out tomorrow."

"All thanks to you," I said, taking her hand and pulling

her down. She came easily and her kiss was warm and gentle. When she sat up to get her breath, I felt faint stirrings where no stir had stirred for a few days. "You know," I said, "that because you've saved my life you now have an obligation to care for me. I'm now your responsibility."

"I'm Portuguese, not Chinese or Japanese or Korean or whatever nationality it was that spawned the thinker of that famous thought. The way we Occidentals figure it, you owe me."

"How much?"

"This much, for a start." She leaned down again and stayed awhile. My faint stirrings stirred some more.

"You're getting better, all right." Zee grinned, glancing down the bed. She got up and moved to a chair. "I think I'll sit over here. I don't want you to hurt yourself on my account."

"*La Belle Dame sans merci.* I recognized you from the start."

"Well, it's certainly true that you're alone and palely loitering."

"And in thrall, too. I want you to notice that. To you, of course."

"Of course. I wouldn't have it any other way."

Nor would I.

Later, the chief came by to tell me that they'd found the Buick in Menemsha but hadn't found any people to go with it. I wasn't surprised. He also said he'd taken the guard off my room. A waste of money, he said. I had to agree.

The next day Zee came by and took me home. The beach between Oak Bluffs and Edgartown was filled with

June People browning nicely, their cars lining the highway.
Beyond them the sails were white against the blue of sea
and sky. Life!

We bounced slowly down my long driveway and pulled
up to the house. I got out and looked around, leaning on
my cane. The Landcruiser was parked where it belonged.
There was no pile of rotting clams in the front yard. Zee
sat me on one of my lawn chairs, went in, and came out
with a bottle of Samuel Adams beer and a frosted mug.

"Chilled the glass in the freezer just for you," she said,
sitting across the table from me.

The sun was warm and nice. Beyond Zee, my garden
was perking up through the ground. I poured the beer
and took a long drink. Ecstasy! Sam Adams is America's
finest bottled beer. I thanked Zee for cleaning the place
up. She bowed her head slightly and smiled. I had some
more beer. When the bottle was empty, Zee brought me
another one and one for herself and some crackers and
cheddar and smoked bluefish. She pulled her chair
around beside mine and we ate and drank beer and
looked over the garden at the blue Sound. The sailboats
leaned distantly in the wind and walked over the dark
water. Cape Pogue lighthouse was a tiny white line against
the sky.

"So Billy never showed up," said Zee when we were on
our next beers.

"Not that I heard."

"Do you want me to get your pistol? I found it in the
Landcruiser and put it inside the house."

"No, I don't plan on shooting anybody today. Didn't you
notice? I'm the shootee, not the shooter. Ours is an age of
technological specialization. If a man wants to get ahead

he has to concentrate on his area of expertise. Mine is getting shot. I've been shot by people all over the world. I'm good at it."

"Billy's never been picked up by the police. He may still be around somewhere, but you're not worried. Why not?"

"I've been thinking. Always a dangerous experience for me, I know, but I've risked it."

"Don't clown."

"All right." I pulled off my shirt and let the sun shine on my scars. It felt good.

"I think they've deep-sixed Billy," I said.

"Who?"

"Sylvia's crowd. They took him out to sea in the *Bluefin* and dropped him overboard with something heavy attached. They looked for him all night, and when they found him up in Chilmark they took him with them to Menemsha and they all went aboard the *Bluefin* and off they went. Mrs. Sylvia, too."

"The *Bluefin* isn't back yet. Nobody seems to know where it is."

"It's fast and it's got a great cruising range, so it could be anywhere between here and the Carolinas. It could be at the bottom of the ocean for that matter, but I doubt it. I think it will be back with everybody but Billy aboard and they'll be surprised as hell to find out the fuzz has been looking for them. If they admit they took Billy aboard at all, they'll say they dropped him off in Point Judith or New Bedford or somewhere and haven't seen him since. Then the cops will go over the boat with the same fine-tooth comb they used to go over Sylvia's house and they'll find just exactly the same nothing. There won't be a flake of grass or snow because the boat will have been scrubbed and vacuumed from bilge to mast top. And

Sylvia will walk away just like always. Later, I imagine, he'll arrange to have his computer records—floppy disks or whatever they are—brought back to his office from wherever it is he's got them secreted at the moment, and he'll be back in business just like before. It wouldn't surprise me if they're in a bank vault somewhere. Sylvia, being the good businessman that he is, would want them to be completely secure."

"But why would they kill Billy? He never did anything to them. Why would they even be looking for him, for that matter?"

"It wasn't what he did, it was what they figured he might do."

"What was that?"

"Talk. Spill the beans. Go state's witness in exchange for immunity. He'd testify and they'd go up while he walked away. So they croaked him."

The sun burned down and sweat began to gather under my chin and run down over my chest. I was dotted with red spots and looked like I had the pox.

"Why did they think that Billy would do that? They had no reason." Zee was leaning back, looking at the blue Vineyard sky.

"If they'd had no reason, they'd not have gone after him. But they did go after him. They picked him up in Maria Sylvia's car. They delayed their departure in the *Bluefin* while they looked for him. As soon as they got him, they left."

Zee was watching a sea gull floating on the high wind. "But why did they think he'd talk. Why did they think he'd testify against them?"

"Because he said he would. I've got a tape of him saying that he would."

"Yeah, but they don't know that. Nobody knows but you."

"Wrong. I gave a copy of the tape to the chief in Edgartown. We played it in his office."

"Oh, come on, Jefferson, you surely don't think that the chief tipped off Sylvia!"

"No, I don't think he did it. . . ."

"Who, then?"

"Helen Viera."

"Ah, what a fool I am. I should have guessed. Who's Helen Viera?"

"Helen Viera is a desk cop in Edgartown. There have been leaks to the bad guys before, and the local cops began to figure that somebody close to them was talking to the other side, but they haven't been able to figure out who it was. It was hard to figure because there are so many independent police departments on this island that security is hard to maintain. Just on this little island we've got the Edgartown Police, the Oak Bluffs Police, the Vineyard Haven Police, the West Tisbury Police, the Chilmark Police, the Gay Head Police, the Sheriff's Department, and the State Police, to say nothing of the DEA or whatever other state or federal outfits that might be involved in, say, a drug bust. That's a lot of cops and cops' girlfriends and boyfriends and wives and husbands and friends of wives and husbands and girlfriends and boyfriends—the security leak could be anywhere.

"Look at this case, for instance. I knew a guy in Boston who had some contacts with the Boston cops. Somebody owed him a favor and gave him information about when this latest bust was going down. The cop trusted my guy and my guy trusted me, and if I'd wanted to, I could have tipped Sylvia myself. I didn't, but Sylvia found out anyway. Just in time—by the skin of his teeth, almost—to grab his records and take a boat ride and to take Billy away at the same time."

Zee was watching me. I thought she looked sleepy and particularly sensual. "But why do you think it was Helen Viera?" she asked. "If she's been the double agent all along, why hasn't she been caught before. The cops aren't fools, after all."

"Because this time she didn't just tip off Fred Sylvia about the time of the bust, she also tipped him off about Billy threatening to squeal on Maria Sylvia. The only people who knew about that threat were Billy himself, me, and whoever listened to that tape. The only person I played that tape for was the chief, but if Helen Viera has ears as sharp as I imagine she has, and if she keeps them as open as I think she does, she could have listened through the chief's door and heard the whole tape. It had to be her."

"You have a nice bod," said Zee. "It's pretty sorry-looking right now, I'll admit, but on the other side of those bullet holes I'll bet it's not bad at all. Why do you think she tipped anybody off?"

"You have a nice-looking exterior yourself which I wouldn't mind exploring in further detail, but I want to impress you with the beauty and clarity of my mind so you won't just think I'm only another empty-headed Greek god type, so try to keep your hands off me while I babble on."

"I'll have my crew tie me to the mast as I listen to your siren song. Consider me tied." She lay back and crossed her wrists above her head. Her breasts announced their freedom from the restriction of a bra. After what seemed a while, I cleared my throat and went on:

"I think she tipped them off for the same reason even honest people tell secrets—because she has lots of loyalties and her loyalty to the police force is only one of them. I think she tipped them off because everybody on this island seems to be related to everybody else or knows everybody else and she didn't want some friend or relative to get arrested. I think that's what they'll find out when they question her. Helen's a perfectly nice person, and as far as I know she's always done her work well. Except for this. When they dig around, I think somebody with a bad habit will be found in the woodwork, somebody that Helen Viera loves or wants to protect.

"Maybe that someone is Sylvia himself. Maybe not. But it was someone close enough to pass the message along in time for Sylvia and company to get away. Before they went, though, they wanted Billy. So did the cops, of course, but the cops were looking for him in his own little sportscar, which smart Billy was no longer driving because he'd borrowed his pal Tim Mello's red M.G. Sylvia, on the other hand, knew what Billy was driving because, no doubt, Tim Mello told him. That made it easier for the Sylvia gang to find Billy, and that's what they did. They used Maria's car because they knew the cops would be hunting for Fred's black Caddy. When they found Billy he was in bad shape and probably ready to go anywhere to get away from the fuzz and you and your fishing rod. That was a great cast, by the way. I don't think I'll ever forget it."

"Can you walk?"

"I think so."

"Watch this, then." She pulled her wrists apart and

swung her feet to the ground. "Ulysses bursts her bonds."
She took my arm. "Ulysses leaps from the ship and seizes
the slightly cratered siren and drags him into a cave and
slams the door."

We got up and walked into the house.

"Do caves have doors?"

"Who cares," said Zee.

* 22 *

Zee's hair was blue-black and it fell like raven's wings, like liquid night, over her shoulders when she unpinned it. It flowed out over the pillow, rich and thick, dark lava, framing her fair face in a black sunburst. Her skin was smooth and fine textured, and her body was sleek as a sea otter. In my arms she was earth and air, fire and water. She rippled and burned, felt light as ether, deep as the earth. We tangled like vines, ebbed and flowed like the tides, then rose and rose to some peak where I'd not been before and there exploded into space and fell and fell until the earth came back and the Vineyard swirled out of the timeless sea and we were entwined together once again on my bed, hot and slick and smelling of sex.

Zee's head was on my chest, her hair a great swirling black stream tumbling over my face, over her white shoulders and back. She pushed herself up on her elbows and her rose-tipped breasts touched my chest. I cupped them in my hands.

"Well," said Zee, smiling down. "Well, well." She sank back down and I put my arms around her.

"By and large," I said finally, "this beats beer and bluefish pâté."

She laughed and snuggled down a bit more. I ran my

hands down her back. Her strong hips flared out from her waist in a silken flow, and as my hands explored her she moved those hips and I felt the faint stirrings of resurrecting life.

Zee's voice came from somewhere beneath the dark weight of her hair: "Madieras to Enterprise, Madieras to Enterprise. I think there's intelligent life on this planet. It isn't dead after all!"

It wasn't. "We should call him Phoenix," said Zee later. "He rose from his own ashes."

"And he'll do it again," I said. "But I think it may take him longer than it did before."

"Shall we wait here or go outside and sit in the sun?"

We went out. It was midafternoon. The warm sun slanted down and the yard was warm. I wore my bathrobe and Zee wore a sheet. We abandoned both and lay in the sun.

"Not too long," said Zee sleepily. "You'll burn something you don't want to burn."

Fifteen minutes later she was sleeping. I covered her with the sheet so she wouldn't burn anything *she* didn't want burned and got myself a beer. I drank the beer and looked at Zee. I watched her until finally she awoke, marveling at her, feeling tender and protective toward her, wondering if she'd stay with me that night.

She did.

The next morning she left early so she could drive home and change before going to work.

"Bring some clothes here," I said. "Stay here. I'll cook and really be a terrific companion. Wait till I get over being shot. You ain't seen nothing yet."

She kissed me, shook her head, and smiled. "Not yet. I'm not sure I want to live with anybody yet."

"You might not want to live here, but it's a great place to visit."

She laughed. "It is that, Jefferson. I've got to go."

"When will I see you?"

"How about tonight?"

"How about that! Forget what I said about the clothes. I like you just as well without them."

"Good-bye, Jefferson. Have the martinis cold about six."

"Trust me."

I watched her drive out of sight and up the road. I felt good, better than I could remember feeling. Except for my sore spots, of course, but they didn't feel important anymore. I went inside and smelled the sheets, then made the bed and washed up the breakfast dishes. Outside, it was a beautiful day. Another beautiful day on beautiful Martha's Vineyard.

I got dressed and drove down to the Edgartown Police station. Helen Viera was at the desk. She smiled at me and seemed pleased that I was getting better. She told me that the chief was downtown directing traffic. Where else, on a summer's day in Edgartown? Drug busts come and go, but traffic is forever. I limped downtown and found the chief at the four corners telling a driver from New Jersey how to get to South Beach. I leaned against the wall of the bank and waited. After a while a young summer cop came down the street, and the chief put him in charge of answering dumb questions and came over.

"Let's go for a walk," I said.

We went along South Summer Street, took a right on Davis Lane and another right on Church Street and another back on Main and came down to the four corners again. By that time I'd told him what I thought about Helen Viera.

He looked rather grim and pale. "I'll check it out," he said in a thin voice. "I hate to think you might be right, but you might."

"I hope I'm wrong."

"Yeah."

As I drove home, I didn't feel as good as I had earlier. It was almost noon by the time I reached the house and the sun was hot. I had some lunch washed down with the last Sam Adams in the house, put on a bathing suit, and went outside to rest in the sun. After a while I nodded off. When I woke up, there was a little puddle of sweat pooled in my belly button. Cute. I got up and the small sea spilled down across my skin.

Over the greening garden I could see the Sound dotted with boats. It was a lovely and innocent scene, one I liked very much. It was the way I preferred to envision Martha's Vineyard: sun, sand, and sails; shellfish and bluefish; cocktail parties attended by casual, tanned people, the women in white or pastel dresses, the men in slacks, alligator shirts, and boat shoes; beach parties with beer kegs and hot dogs and the smell of grass.

The Chamber of Commerce island was the one I liked. But there was another one, too, the one of big dirty money and fast times and violence and stupidity, of drugs and death and lies and deceit. And it was almost as real, maybe just as real, or even more real than the other one.

I thought that the worlds we live in are pretty insular, pretty isolated from other worlds that occupy the same time and space that we do. Summer sailors live in a world that is almost unknown to the fishermen whose boats move over the same waters. Those of us who fish Wasque have neither contact nor interest with the sunbathers and swimmers who share South Beach with us. Policemen know nothing of the lives of schoolteachers and vice versa.

I thought of the many little worlds there were on the Vineyard and how it was that occasionally someone like me would be nudged out of his normal comfortable niche into another life he'd not normally even notice. Such experience gives you a double vision, makes you aware of things you'd normally not see, makes your life a bit chancier than it usually seems.

I wasn't sure the new knowledge was worth it. Better, maybe, not to have the Janus face, not to see both yin and yang, the dark and the light. Better, maybe, to see only the sloop leaning across the summer wind and not to see Billy Martin coshing Jim Norris with a blunt object, then blowing up the *Nellie Grey*, or not to see, right now, Billy's own body turning in the watery winds of the sea, legs attached to something heavy lying on the ocean bottom. Fish nibbled, shark bit, lobster sampled? Hair waving in the green wind, eyes of pearl, coral for bones, full fathom five.

There isn't a consistent justice in the world, although it does sometimes occur. Sometimes the bomber gets blown up by his own bomb; sometimes the thief is bitten by the cobra he's stolen; sometimes God seems to take a hand. As often as not, though, the universe is indifferent to the things men count as important, and the bad guys do just fine, thanks. No surprise, then, that Sylvia and company slipped away cleanly, for nature does not share man's insistence that the right prevail; by natural law, the prevailer is in the right; if the deer escapes the lion, the deer is in the right; if the lion kills the deer, the lion is in the right. Of all species, only man seems offended by this.

But I am a man and I was offended by Billy and by Sylvia and his kind. And I wanted justice and thought that it should prevail. Chesterton argued that children, being innocent, prefer justice, while adults, being sinners, prefer love. I had cut myself off from both love and justice for a time, but now I wanted both back again. I saw in Zee the promise of love and wished that I could create it in her somehow. But that I could not do. I could love her, but I couldn't make her love me. On the other hand, I might manage justice of a sort.

Billy, if my guess was right, had already received his dose; he shared the sea with the remains of the *Nellie Grey.* Sylvia, however, looked free and clear. Not much I could do about that unless he came back.

I glanced at the sun and then at my watch. It was one of those two-dollar ones you get at the gas station when you fill her up. I like them. They keep good time and you don't mind when you forget and go swimming with them and they stop. Then you just get a new one. This one had a calendar function. It had been exactly two weeks since the *Nellie Grey* had blown up. Two weeks since I'd first seen Zee. A lot had happened. I went inside and phoned Susie Martin.

I'd thawed out some of last fall's oysters and was laying out a cookie pan of oysters Rockefeller when Susie arrived. I gave her a Coke, got a Molson for myself, and we went outside and sat in the light of the westering sun.

"Susie, do you still play tennis at the club?"

She cocked her head, then nodded.

"I need to know what Maria Sylvia has in her locker there. I can't get into the ladies' locker room, but you can. I want you to empty out her locker and bring the contents to me. After I have a look, I want you to put the stuff back."

"I can't do that. I don't have a key to her padlock."

"I'll give you an athletic bag. It'll have a new padlock and a pair of chain cutters in it. I want you to cut her padlock, put her stuff in the athletic bag, put the new padlock on her locker, then bring the bag of stuff to me."

She twisted her Coke can. "Has this got anything to do with Billy? Where is he, anyhow? The police don't know a thing."

"It might have something to do with Billy. I have to see the material in the locker before I'll know. Will you help me?"

"What do you think you'll find? What has it got to do with my brother?"

"If I find anything, I'll tell you then. If I don't, I won't."

She glanced at her watch. "I'll go about six o'clock, then. Most people are home for supper. The locker room should be pretty empty. How do you work the chain cutters?"

I brought the athletic bag from the shed out back and showed her how to use the cutters.

"Something's happened to Billy, hasn't it?" she asked.

"I don't know."

"Don't lie, J.W."

"I won't. I have a guest coming over this evening, so I won't be able to see you until tomorrow morning. Can you bring the stuff by about eight A.M.?"

"Something *has* happened, hasn't it?"

"I think so. I'll talk to you tomorrow when you bring the stuff here. Don't get caught. One other thing—wear gloves."

She drove away, a pretty girl who shouldn't be introduced to the dark mysteries quite so soon in life.

I set the table with a white cloth and my best stainless steel. My only stainless steel, in fact. I put both my matching wineglasses and my best plates across from each other. Zee and I would be able to sigh at one another over the candles I'd found in the Big D the year before and had been saving for just the right occasion.

Zee's arrival made it just the right occasion. I served icy vodka martinis on the balcony, where we admired the view of the sea and watched the late boats easing toward Edgartown.

"A Babar day," I said.

"A what?"

"A Babar day. Remember Babar the elephant? There's a picture in one of the Babar books of a beach covered with people and umbrellas and the ocean full of boats and such. I think maybe Babar is floating over it in a balloon or something. Anyway, it's all bright and clean and perfect, just the way a scene like that should be. It looks like that out there right now. Sharp colors, just the right number of boats doing just the right things, just the right cars and people on their way home from the beach. Just the right-colored sky and water. A Babar day."

"Right," said Zee. "I remember that picture."

Another link between us—Babar the elephant.

After two martinis (no more lest the taste buds become dulled) we went below and I served the oysters with vinho verde. When the last oyster had been devoured, I cleared the table and we took coffee, apples and cheese, and Cognac out onto the porch where we could sit in the soft evening breeze and look out over garden and Sound.

Zee sat beside me and our shoulders touched. I felt a thrill and a sense of contentment at the same time. I took her hand.

"Not bad," said Zee. "Not bad at all. I think this is the way it's supposed to be. Woman comes home from a hard day at the office, finds martinis waiting, an elegant supper, a dutiful stud, a soft summer night."

"It's the American way."

She turned and kissed me. After a while we took the Cognac and sat in the yard and watched the stars come out. Then we went to bed and it was indeed the way it's supposed to be.

Zee was gone when Susie arrived the next morning. I stopped washing dishes and we sat in the living room.

"Any trouble?"

She shook her head. I put on a pair of cotton gardening gloves and went over Maria Sylvia's gear. I found mostly the normal stuff I expected to find—a sweater, some clean socks and sundry toiletries, two tennis rackets and a can of balls, wristbands and a headband, a clean towel, odds and ends. I also found a little purse containing vials of liquid similar to that I'd taken off Julie Potter and a packet of pills that looked like the Dexamyl I'd seen years before in Boston. Dex for up, the codeine to mellow out.

"What's going on?" asked Susie. "You said you'd tell me."

"Wait." I went out to the shed again and brought in the drugs I'd gotten from Julie and Billy. I put them in the athletic bag along with Maria Sylvia's gear.

"I think Billy's dead," I said. "I think Maria Sylvia killed him or had it done."

When Susie could listen to more, I gave it to her.

* 23 *

I told her about Maria and her young men, and about what Julie had said to me—that Billy was dealing at Brown but his source was named Sylvia. "It wasn't Billy's buddy Danny, because he was in California, and it wasn't Danny's old man because his old man only merchandises the stuff. Like a lot of criminal types, he wants his own kids to keep their hands cleaner than his are. It's a kind of paternalism you run into in crime, a conservative streak. The old man's more interested in business and teacups than in his wife, but she's a hungry woman still and she likes a vigorous life. So she deals dope to keep the boys coming. The stuff in the locker is the same as the stuff I took off Julie, and Julie got it from Billy. Maria fed Billy his dope."

"But why would she kill him?"

I told her about Billy being picked up by Maria Sylvia's car and about the *Bluefin* pulling out of Menemsha and Maria's Buick being found there later. When I was done, I looked as honest as I could and said, "She killed him because he was going to testify against her and the whole outfit, just like you thought he might. The police have a tape of him saying he'd testify. Sylvia found out about it and they got him before he could talk."

"No!"

207

"Yes." I tapped the athletic bag. "And they'll get away with it, too, because there'll be no evidence against them, especially not against her. That's why I want this stuff back in her locker. When it's there, I want the police to get a phone tip so they'll go down and find it. That way they'll have that much on her at least, if she ever decides to come back to the island."

She cried for a while in that terrible way young women can cry, and she said, "I knew it! I knew it! First they tried to kill him on the *Nellie Grey* and then they finally did it. Poor Billy, poor Billy. He was screwed up for such a long time. But he finally was going to do the right thing, wasn't he?"

"Yeah," I lied, "he was finally going to do the right thing."

"I'll put this gear back in her locker," she said. "And I'll phone the tip in to the police, too. Nobody will see me at her locker and nobody will recognize my voice on the phone, either. I want to do it!"

Chesterton was right: children, being innocent, prefer justice.

"Be careful," I said. "Remember you're doing something very illegal, something you may want to talk about sometime but won't be able to."

"I know. J.W.?"

"Yeah?"

"You did what I asked you to do. It's worse than I thought it could ever be, but I'm glad you did it and I'm glad you told me the truth, even though it's awful. It's important that Billy was finally trying to do the right thing."

"I know. That's why I told you."

When she had gone, I went in and looked at the tide

clock. The east tide had just started. High tide would be at one in the afternoon. I wondered if I could cast. The idea of fresh bluefish for supper appealed to me. Zee would be impressed. Annoyed, too, since I'd have gotten it while she was working. Not a bad prospect, all in all. I finished the dishes, straightened up the house, and got everything loaded into the Landcruiser. It was another hot day, so I wore shorts and sandals and a T-shirt that said ALL MY PARENTS BROUGHT BACK FROM TWO WEEKS ON MARTHA'S VINEYARD WAS THIS BLEEPING SHIRT. I put beer and sandwiches into the cooler and was on my way.

Edgartown was a traffic cop's nightmare in front of the A&P, as usual, but once I got by all the people making left turns I was all right. I picked up two kids, a boy and a girl obviously of the working-on-the-island-between-semesters sort, and took them both to South Beach. They eyed my holey hide with curiosity but were too polite to ask what all the damage meant.

After I dropped them off, I drove east along the beach. The clammers were out on the flats in Katama Bay, kites were flying brightly against the pale blue sky, lifted by the gentle southwestern wind, and the beach was lined with Jeeps and sun bathers. I drove past them all, over the golden sand to Wasque Point. It was Tuesday, and there were a dozen pickups and wagons there before me. Nobody was fishing. They were between fish. I found a gap in the line of cars and pulled in.

I had a beer and looked out toward where Nantucket was supposed to be. Too much humidity to see Muskeget today. Instead, a hazy horizon with the sea blending into the sky. Now and then someone would walk down to the surf and make a few casts, but no one caught anything. I wondered if Sylvia would come back. Why not? He might be a suspect, but nobody had any proof. He was a legitimate businessman, after all. Of course he wouldn't know about the drugs found in his wife's locker until he got back, and that might surprise him into making some sort of slip. Or maybe the cops could pressure Maria into talking about where she got her supply. I wondered. Life is an ambiguous proposition at times.

Out in the water, at about the end of my normal cast, I thought I saw a change in the surface. I squinted at it, then got out and took down my rod. I had on a three-ounce Roberts. I walked down and made my cast. It hurt, but the graphite cooperated. The plug arched out and down into the shimmering water. As the plug hit the water, the bluefish hit the plug in an explosion of spray. I set the hook and the rod arched. Instantly there were fishermen on both sides of me. Some things in life are dependable after all.

I had the fish ready for the oven when Zee drove in. She was somber.

"What's happened?" I asked.

"I had George's nitroglycerin tablets analyzed," she said. "They're placebos."

Why wasn't I surprised? Because patricide seemed no worse than fratricide? No less surprising or ominous? Maybe because Billy had seemed quite mad when last I'd seen him and his madness did not seem brand new? Who understood such dark purposes as those which moved Billy to act as he did? Freud? Dostoyevsky? Certainly not I. All I knew was that it was a secret probably best not revealed to the Martin family. Not ever.

I took Zee's hand and we went into the kitchen and I showed her the supper I'd caught. Later, after we'd eaten and were sitting on the porch over coffee, we talked a long time and watched the moon rise over the Sound. The stars came out and the wind sighed through the trees. It was a lovely, soft summer night. Finally we went to bed and held one another until we slept.

The next day I shipped Jim's ring to Oregon.